OLIVER TWISTED

OLIVER TWISTED

Or The Witch Boy's Progress

J D SHARPE

(and Charles Dickens)

Published in Great Britain in 2012
by Electric Monkey an imprint of Egmont UK Limited
239 Kensington High Street
London W8 6SA

Text copyright © 2012 J D Sharpe
The moral rights of the author have been asserted

ISBN 978 1 4052 5817 3

1 3 5 7 9 10 8 6 4 2

www.electricmonkeybooks.co.uk

A CIP catalogue record for this title is available from the British Library

Typeset by Avon Dataset Ltd, Bidford on Avon, Warwickshire
Printed and bound in Great Britain by the CPI Group

48753/1

MIX
Paper
FSC   FSC® C018306

EGMONT

Our story began over a century ago, when seventeen-year-old
Egmont Harald Petersen found a coin in the street. He was on
his way to buy a flyswatter, a small hand-operated printing
machine that he then set up in his tiny apartment.

The coin brought him such good luck that today Egmont has
offices in over 30 countries around the world. And that lucky
coin is still kept at the company's head offices in Denmark.

For Stella, for taking a punt . . .

Chapter I

Which tells of Oliver Twisted's birth

In a certain town, which for many reasons it will be prudent to refrain from mentioning, there is one building anciently common to most towns, great or small: the workhouse.

And in this workhouse was born, on a day and date which I need not trouble myself to repeat, a boy who, according to fortune-tellers and oracles alike, would be our true defender, the protector who would one day close hell's mouth forever – ending the darkness that had sunk deep into the heart of the kingdom.

And yet, with another cast of their gnarly divination bones, the same soothsayers, with furrowed brows and low voices, prophesied a very different future – the same boy would grow up to become the greatest evil ever known.

A boy with two possible destinies.

A boy whose name is prefixed to this here book.

For a long time after Oliver Twisted was ushered into this sorrowful world by the village surgeon, it remained a matter of considerable doubt whether the child would survive to bear any name at all. The fact is, there was considerable difficulty in convincing Oliver to take upon himself the office of respiration – a troublesome practice, but one which custom has made necessary to our survival unless you are of vampyric extraction and stopped breathing long ago.

For some time, the baby lay gasping on a little flock mattress, rather unequally poised between this world and the next: the balance being decidedly in favour of the latter. Now if, during this brief period, Oliver had been surrounded by black-tongued ghouls or a clan of pit demons, he would most inevitably have been killed in no time, and his baby-soft flesh picked clean off his bones.

There being nobody by, however, but an old pauper woman, who was rendered rather misty by an unexpected allowance of beer, and a surgeon, who was also the village's only butcher, Oliver and Nature fought out the point between them. And Fate set her game between good and evil into beautiful, terrible motion. The result being that, after a few struggles, Oliver breathed, sneezed and then set up a cry as loud as a harpooned harpy.

As Oliver gave this first proof of the free and proper action of his lungs, the patchwork coverlet, which was carelessly flung over the iron bedstead, rustled, and the pretty but pale face of the young woman who was his mother was raised feebly from the pillow. 'Let me see my child before I die,' she said faintly.

The surgeon, who had taken the squalling newborn over to the fire to examine it better, advanced to the bed's head. 'Oh, you must not talk about dying yet,' he said, with more kindness than might have been expected of him.

The patient looked at the surgeon with haunted, emerald-coloured eyes. 'There is no escaping destiny, Doctor.' She stretched out her hand towards her child and the doctor deposited him in her arms.

The young woman imprinted her cold white lips passionately on the baby's forehead. 'My son, my very own heart,' she whispered. 'Your path will not be easy – my runes have shown me that. But you must stand straight in the face of evil.' She turned her head and coughed violently – flecks of blood rained down on the bed's worn coverlet. Her expression became wild as she looked back at her baby. 'You have the power to save us all. You must.'

'Be calm, dear girl,' the surgeon soothed. 'You know not what you say. Rest now.'

The woman drew her hand across the crimson that wetted her mouth and kissed her son again. She squeezed her eyes shut as an awful trembling took over her body. 'Take him.' Her voice was low and rough. 'Take him from me before I kill him.'

'Lor bless your dear heart, no!' interposed the old nurse from the corner of the room. She hastily deposited a glass beer bottle in her pocket. 'You must not take on in this way.'

The old woman reached down and took the wriggling baby in her arms. 'Rest, rest, like the good doctor 'ere said.' She held the swaddled baby close to her bony chest, her face folding into familiar lines of sorrow. 'And dearest, listen, it ain't mothers who kill their children – that work is left to others.' The nurse's mouth drew inwards like a purse pulled shut. 'I had thirteen children of my own, and all of 'em dead except two, and them in the workhouse with me. It won't be long till they're taken by the Brotherhood and sacri –'

The nurse broke off as the young woman suddenly bucked in the bed, froth joining the blood on her lips. Her skin shone maggot-white in the low firelight, then rippled and thinned, showing the contours of her skull.

'There is not much time,' the young woman gasped

out. 'You must get away from me. I'm infected.' With each word uttered, blue veins raced across her face, like fissures of mould on cave-ripened cheese.

'Lor preserve us.' The old nurse stepped back. The veins in the young woman's face were pulsing with such violence it was as if a clew of worms was trying to break through the skin. The nurse held the warm bulk of the baby closer to her body. 'Doctor, there's somethink very wrong 'ere,' she wailed.

'I-I was b-bitten, on the road,' the young mother stuttered out. 'I couldn't run fast enough and all my power was gone.' She sobbed and pulled back her sleeve to reveal an ugly-looking wound which oozed with custard-thick pus.

'You were bitten by one of the woe-begottens?' The doctor's voice was reed-thin. He gagged as he tasted decay in the back of his throat – the foul stench of spoiling meat wafted up from the infected woman and filled the small room.

The girl nodded. 'I held back the change for as long as I could.' She gritted her teeth as another convulsion went through her and sores bloomed on her face. 'I needed to know that my baby would be born untainted.' A cry left her lips as a ridge of angry blisters erupted on the crown of her head. Clumps of her soft golden hair fell on to the bed – curls streaked with blood.

'Doctor, do somethink!' the nurse shrieked. 'Kill 'er before she kills us.' The old woman held out the baby in front of her like a shield. 'Lor preserve us, you know what a woe-begotten can do. Once she's changed, she'll snap us in half, she'll pluck the eyeballs from our heads and suck the jelly right out of 'em.'

The baby in her arms began to wail.

The doctor tried to move his feet, but fear had staked them to the floor. He could only stare at the creature on the bed in horror. He'd known them to have many names: the cursed, zombies, woe-begottens. But only one name was truly correct – killers.

The young woman's small hand clenched the bedsheet as another shudder went through her body, a plain wedding ring gleaming. Her green irises flooded with yellow. 'T-take c-care of my baby. He is more important than you know.' Her shaking hand reached to her throat and ripped at the golden locket that rested there. Flicking it open, she took a tiny vial of liquid from its interior and quickly gulped it down.

The doctor watched as the woman's fingers went into spasm and then released the glass vial. It rolled across the bed and smashed as it struck the floor.

The young mother gasped and then sighed. Her yellow eyes seemed to fill with peace. She lifted a hand out to her child. 'I will always be with you,' she whispered. She then passed her palms over her face, fell back and died.

The room was eerily silent, except for the fire crackling in the grate. Even the child had stopped crying as if shocked into silence. The doctor cautiously edged forward and checked the transformed woe-begotten's hands and temples, but the blood had stopped forever.

He knelt and picked up a shard of the glass vial. The scent of almonds instantly assailed his nostrils. 'Dragon's blood,' he murmured.

'Is it all over then, doctor?' the nurse asked with a sniff.

The surgeon nodded. 'The brave girl poisoned herself.' His brow creased in puzzlement. 'But where she obtained dragon's blood, I'll never know. It is as rare to find as a friendly gorgon.'

The nurse looked at the dead woman. 'Ah, poor dear, so it is!' She checked to make sure the doctor wasn't looking and then scooped up the golden locket that had fallen out on the pillow and dropped it into her pocket. 'Poor, poor dear!'

'You needn't mind sending for me if the child sickens, nurse,' said the surgeon, putting on his gloves with great deliberation. 'It's very likely it *will* be troublesome – a wild child, tainted by the woe-begotten bite.' He sighed deeply. 'But she asked us to take care of him and so I will not dispose of him.'

He put on his hat and, pausing by the bedside on his

way to the door, added, 'She was a good-looking girl too. Where did she come from?'

'She was brought here last night,' replied the old woman. 'Poor dear was found lying in the street. She must have walked some distance for her shoes were worn to pieces, but where she came from, or where she was going to, is anybody's guess.'

The surgeon leant over the body and looked at the woe-begotten bite, now red and puckered against the dead woman's greying skin. 'The old story,' he said, shaking his head. 'A traveller, journeying alone, completely defenceless when the horde of devil creatures attack. I wish I did not have to see these things. Ah! The world we live in, 'tis truly a place of darkness. Goodnight!'

The medical gentleman walked away to dinner and the nurse, having once more applied herself to the beer bottle, sat down on a low chair before the fire and proceeded to dress the infant.

What an excellent example of the power of dress young Oliver Twisted was! Wrapped in the simple blanket, he might have been the child of a vampyre nobleman or a beggar. But now that he was dressed in yellow, stained rags, he fell into place at once – an orphan of the workhouse, despised by all and pitied by none.

Oliver cried lustily. If he could have known that he was an orphan, left to the tender mercies of the dark world, perhaps he would have cried the louder.

Chapter II

Where Oliver grows up

The Brotherhood, who ran the workhouse magnanimously and humanely, resolved that Oliver should be 'farmed'. In other words, that he should be dispatched to a bloodfarm some three miles off, where twenty or thirty other juvenile unfortunates resided without the inconvenience of too much food or too much clothing, under the parental superintendence of an elderly matron called Mrs Mann.

This good lady would drain Oliver and his companions each day of a pint of blood for the vampyre gentry of the parish. For it is well known that the vampyric upper classes abhor hunting children, but find their blood to be the stickiest and sweetest.

The instruments of drainage were simple enough: gargantuan leeches which Mrs Mann would affix to the throats of the children on her farm. Once the leeches were plump and round with blood, she would pack the creatures away in straw and stack the precious cargo on the blood waggon ready for its morning run to the great houses of the parish.

The old matron received sevenpence-halfpenny per small head per week. A great deal may be got for sevenpence-halfpenny, quite enough to overload a child's stomach and make it uncomfortable. The elderly female knew what was good for children, but she had an even better idea of what was good for herself – so she took the greater part of the weekly payment for her own use.

Unfortunately for Mrs Mann, in eight and a half cases out of ten, the children died from want and cold, or fell into the fire from neglect, or were half-smothered by accident. In most of these cases, the miserable little beings were usually summoned to the next world. To their delight, they found it to be a blissful place. Even the ones that went to the fiery realm were jovial for they found it to be airy and spacious as a good deal of the creatures that used to live there had escaped their bonds and now resided above ground.

Occasionally, and very annoyingly, Mrs Mann's pay would be docked for damaging the livestock when a farmed child turned up as a blue corpse, or was inadvertently scalded to death when there happened to be a bathing day. It is true though that the latter accident was very scarce as bath day only happened when the farm was to be visited by the vampyric gentry . . .

Still, these noble men and women would make pilgrimages to the farm to feed on the orphans in person, if only very rarely, but they always sent the beadle the day before to say they were coming. The children were neat and clean to behold when the vampyres arrived, and what more would the vampyres desire than a hygienic meal!

It cannot be expected that this system of farming would produce a very extraordinary or luxuriant crop. Oliver Twisted's twelfth birthday found him a pale, thin child, somewhat diminutive in stature and decidedly small in circumference. But nature or inheritance had implanted a good, sturdy spirit in Oliver's breast. It had had plenty of room to expand, thanks to the lean diet of the establishment.

Be this as it may, however, it was his twelfth birthday and he was locked up in the coal-cellar for outrageously trying to escape from a lengthy and rather painful leeching process.

Upstairs, Mrs Mann was unexpectedly startled by the appearance of Mr Bumble, the beadle, striving to undo the garden gate.

'Goodness gracious! Is that you, Mr Bumble, sir?'

said Mrs Mann, thrusting her head out of the window. 'Susan, take that brat Oliver upstairs and wash him directly,' she hissed over her shoulder to her maid. 'My heart alive! Mr Bumble, how glad I am to see you, surely!'

Now Mr Bumble was a fat man and bad-tempered (some said he'd been pinched by a boggart as a child and so would always be miserable) therefore, instead of returning Mrs Mann's greeting, he gave the little wicket gate a tremendous shake and then bestowed upon it a kick which could have emanated from no leg but a beadle's.

'Lor, only think,' said Mrs Mann, running out, 'that I should have forgotten that the gate was bolted on the inside, on account of them dear children. We wouldn't want them getting away! Walk in, Mr Bumble, do, sir.'

Although this invitation was accompanied with a curtsey, it by no means mollified the beadle.

'Do you think this respectful or proper conduct, Mrs Mann,' enquired Mr Bumble, grasping his cane, 'to keep myself, a representative of the Brotherhood of Fenris, and with an important message from the great and respected Dracula family, waiting at your garden gate?'

'No, sir,' replied the old lady.

'The Dracula family are intent on coming here later today to feed upon your orphans. Are you aware, Mrs

Mann, that you and I are paid well to serve their needs and tend this farm?'

'I'm sure, Mr Bumble, that I was tardy to reach you because I was a-telling one or two of the dear children as is so fond of you that it was you a-coming,' replied Mrs Mann with great humility.

Mr Bumble had a great idea of his own importance and Mrs Mann's words appealed to his vanity. He relaxed.

'Well, well, Mrs Mann,' he replied in a calmer tone. 'Lead the way in, for I come on business and have something to say.'

Mrs Mann ushered the beadle into a small parlour, placed a seat for him and deposited his cocked hat and cane on the table before him. Mr Bumble wiped from his forehead the perspiration resulting from his walk.

'You've had a long walk,' observed Mrs Mann, with captivating sweetness. 'Will you take a little drop of somethink, Mr Bumble?'

'Not a drop. Nor a drop,' said Mr Bumble, waving his right hand in a dignified but placid manner.

'I think you will,' said Mrs Mann, who had noticed the tone of the refusal. 'Just a leetle drop, with some cold water and a lump of sugar.'

'What is it?' inquired the beadle.

'I'll not deceive you, Mr B, it's troll whisky, a very

fine malt,' replied Mrs Mann as she opened a corner cupboard and took down a bottle and glass. 'I'm obliged to keep it in the house, to put into the blessed infants from time to time. It calms them after their nightmares. You know we cannot have fear souring the blood.'

'Do you really give the children troll whisky, Mrs Mann?' enquired Mr Bumble, following the old matron's movements as she mixed the drink.

'Ah, bless 'em, that I do, expensive as it is,' replied the nurse. 'I couldn't see 'em suffer every night, eyes rolled back in their heads, screaming themselves hoarse, splitting the corners of their mouths.'

'No,' said Mr Bumble approvingly. 'No, you could not. You are a humane woman, Mrs Mann.' He licked his fleshy lips as she set down the glass. 'I shall take an early opportunity of mentioning it to the Dracula family and the Brotherhood.' He drew the drink towards him and gulped down half of it.

'And now about business,' said the beadle, taking out a pink and shiny pixie-skinned wallet. 'The child named Oliver Twisted is twelve years old today and thus his blood is no longer of the required grade for the honourable vampyre families of our parish.'

'Poor Oliver, he'll be exiled from my tender care,' murmured Mrs Mann, dabbing her left eye with the corner of her apron. Inside, she felt like doing a jig. All

Oliver ever did was give her lip and aggravation, but soon he would be gone!

'And notwithstanding the most supernatural exertions on the part of the workhouse and their diviners,' said Mr Bumble, 'we have never been able to discover who is Oliver's father, or what was his mother's name.'

Mrs Mann scratched her filthy head, sending askew her frilly widow's cap. 'How come he has any name at all then?' she asked.

The beadle drew himself up with great pride and said, 'I invented it.'

'You, Mr Bumble?'

'I, Mrs Mann. We name our foundlings in alphabetical order. The last was a S – Savage, I named him. This was a T – Twisted, I named *him*.

More like T for troublemaker, Mrs Mann thought bitterly. 'Why, you're quite a creative gentleman, sir,' she said out loud.

'Well, well,' said the beadle, clearly pleased with the compliment, 'perhaps I may be.' He finished the troll whisky and water, and added, 'Oliver shall return to the workhouse today and come under the Brotherhood's care. I have come out myself to take him there. So let me see him at once.'

'I'll fetch him directly,' said Mrs Mann, leaving the room.

Oliver, having had a good amount of the outer coat of dirt which encrusted him hastily scraped off with a wire brush, was waiting in the hallway with Susan, the maid.

Mrs Mann grabbed his arm. 'Now don't you dare to say anything bad about me to the beadle,' she hissed. 'Or I'll make it worse for the others, I promise.'

'I'm sure the beadle is a busy man,' Oliver replied softly. 'There is not enough time in all of eternity to say all the things that are bad about you.'

Mrs Mann gripped him harder. 'You think I'm evil, Oliver.' Her lips pressed into a thin line. 'My boy, there's evil out there you can't even imagine.'

Yanking him so hard that his elbow clicked, Oliver was led into the room by his benevolent protectress.

'Make a bow to the gentleman, Oliver,' said Mrs Mann.

The boy did as he was told.

'Will you go along with me, Oliver?' said Mr Bumble, in a majestic voice.

Oliver was about to say that he would go along with anybody with great readiness when, glancing upward, he caught sight of Mrs Mann, who had got behind the beadle's chair and was shaking her fist at him with a furious expression. He took the hint at once, for that fist had been too often impressed upon his body.

'Will she go with me?' enquired Oliver.

'No, she can't,' replied Mr Bumble. 'But she'll come and see you sometimes.'

Oliver nodded and had sense enough to pretend great regret at going away. It was not a very difficult matter for the boy to call tears into his eyes. Countless memories of white fangs slashing at his throat or of waking up to meet the glassy stare of an orphan who had died in the night was enough to make his eyes wet.

Mrs Mann gave him a thousand embraces, but what Oliver wanted a great deal more was a piece of bread and butter, lest he should seem too scrawny when he got to the workhouse. He'd heard that a boy needed to have his wits and fists about him if he was to survive.

'Mrs Mann, may I have something to eat?' he asked, his voice somewhat muffled by the old woman's sour-smelling embrace.

He felt a sharp pinch on his ribs, but as Mrs Mann stepped back she was all smiles.

'Why, of course, Oliver.'

'And the rest of the boys?' Oliver pressed. 'They mentioned that they were hungry as well.'

'Of course they should eat,' Mr Bumble boomed. 'The Dracula family like their cattle to be well nourished.' The beadle frowned. 'Why do they go hungry, Mrs Mann?'

The old lady gave a simpering smile, although Oliver could see her hands quivering with the desire to wring his neck. 'It must have slipped my mind to give them their supper. I do apologise.'

Mrs Mann called up her maid and instructed her to bring a slice of bread for Oliver and some supper for the rest of the orphans. The maid did as she was bid, albeit with a very surprised expression on her face.

Soon, with the slice of bread in his hand and a brown cloth cap on his head, Oliver was led away by Mr Bumble from the wretched home where one kind word or look had never lighted the gloom of his infant years. And yet, as the cottage gate closed after him, sorrow made his knees feel weak. Wretched as were the companions in misery he was leaving behind, they were the only friends he had ever known and for the first time he had a sense of his loneliness in the great wide world.

Chapter III

In which Oliver meets the Brotherhood of
Fenris and is driven to Desperate Lengths

Mr Bumble walked on with long strides, firmly grasping Oliver's wrist. The boy jogged beside him, enquiring at the end of every quarter of a mile whether they were 'nearly there'. To these interrogations Mr Bumble returned very brief and snappish replies, until they finally reached their destination.

Oliver had not been within the walls of the workhouse a quarter of an hour, and had scarcely completed the demolition of a second slice of bread, when Mr Bumble, who had handed him over to the care of an old woman called Mrs Corney, returned. Telling him it was a live board night, he informed Oliver that the board had requested to see him forthwith.

Not having a very clearly defined notion of what a live board was, Oliver was nonetheless relieved that he was not appearing before a living-dead board. For the last time he encountered someone from that race, the bald-headed fiend, in her expensive garments and fine shoes, had almost torn out his throat in her eagerness to feed.

Oliver had no time to think about the matter, however, for Mr Bumble gave him a tap on the head with his cane, to wake him up, and another on the back, to make him lively. Then, bidding him to follow, the beadle conducted him into a large whitewashed room, where a stone altar stood at the feet of a giant statue of a wolf. Both the altar and the claws of the stone wolf glistened with red and the smell of iron lay heavy in the air.

In the middle of the room, nine fat gentlemen sat round a table. At the head of the table, seated in a chair rather higher than the rest, was another gentleman whose skin hung on his wasted frame, his face as hard and grey as rock.

'Bow to the board,' said Mr Bumble. Oliver, seeing no board but the table, fortunately bowed to that.

'What's your name, boy?' said the gentleman in the raised chair.

Fear gripped Oliver's throat as his gaze caught on the stone wolf and its bloodied altar. 'M-my n-name is –' He faltered as he spotted that many of the men around the table wore a wolf insignia about their necks. He knew from the boys at the bloodfarm that anyone who wore such a symbol worshipped the wolf god, Fenris.

'The Brotherhood of Fenris feast on the hearts of children served on plates of bone,' one boy had said in the dead of night. 'They are more hollow than a skull sucked clean of its brains. They take orphans and lead them to the stone altar and murmur incantations a thousand years old.' The boy's voice became a whisper. 'They slit the ivory of young throats so that they may learn their own futures and avoid death.'

Oliver began to tremble as he looked at the dishes on the table. The plates were bone-white, slightly curved, and something fleshy and red lay pulsing on their surface.

'Answer the high priest, boy.' The beadle gave Oliver a vicious thwack from behind with his cane.

'My name is Oliver Twisted,' he said in a very low and hesitating voice, whereupon a gentleman in a white waistcoat said that Oliver was clearly a simpleton as why else would it take so long for one to say their own name and would it not save time if they simply agreed here and now to sacrifice the boy to Fenris?

'I know not why we insist on this tedious tradition of interviewing an orphan before wielding the sacrificial blade,' the man grumbled.

'Boy,' said the high priest, 'listen to me. You understand that this man wants to sacrifice you to

22

Fenris. You know who Fenris is, I suppose?'

'What's that then, sir?' enquired Oliver, hoping that ignorance might buy him more time.

'The boy *is* a fool – I thought he was,' said the gentleman in the white waistcoat. He wiped his hands on his clothes, smearing them with something scarlet. 'You've made your point. We clearly cannot anger Fenris by sacrificing such an imbecile to him.'

'Hush,' said the high priest. 'Oliver, you know you've got no father or mother, and that you were brought up by Mrs Mann under the jurisdiction of the Dracula family, don't you?'

'Yes, sir,' replied Oliver bitterly.

'Well! That was indeed a great honour to be of service to the noble vampyre families of our parish, but you have been brought here for an even greater honour.' The high priest paused to pick something maroon and juicy from his tomb-like teeth.

Oliver felt the bread and butter that he'd eaten with such relish earlier rise in his throat as he watched the man dig at his black gums with a curved fingernail. 'You must be made ready,' the high priest continued, depositing the stringy discoveries on to his bone plate, 'so that one day you will be fit to be called upon as a sacrifice.' He made a steeple of his bony, long-nailed fingers, stinking spittle making them glisten. 'It is essential that you spend the rest of your time here thinking only the most foul thoughts.' He leant forward. 'Your mind must become as dark as an inkwell. Only by doing this will you be polluted enough for us to offer you up to the mighty Fenris.'

Oliver nodded, but only because a vicious kick from the beadle told him that this was what he should do.

'So you'll begin your education in all things dark and abhorrent tomorrow morning at six o'clock,' added the surly one in the white waistcoat.

Oliver bowed low and was then hurried away to a large ward where, on a rough, hard bed, he hugged himself to keep warm. Poor Oliver! He little thought, as he lay sleeping, that the Brotherhood of Fenris had that very evening made a decision which would exercise the most material influence over all his future fortunes. But they had and this was it:

Starvation.

Starvation of hope.

Starvation of love.

But more importantly, just plain old starvation.

The Brotherhood of Fenris knew that starvation bred desperation, and desperation bred cruelty and deceit. The new system was put into full operation the day after Oliver arrived. And six months later it was deemed to be a great success as the inmates of the workhouse plundered new depths of dark thought and action. Sacrifices to Fenris were plentiful indeed.

Still, the increase in the undertaker's bill and the necessity of taking in the clothes of all the workhouse inmates, which fluttered loosely on their wasted, shrunken forms, meant that the new system had turned out to be a bit more expensive than the Brotherhood would have imagined.

The room in which the workhouse boys were fed once a day was a large stone hall. Long wooden tables lined the space and a copper cauldron stood at one end, out of which the cook, swathed in a large, stained apron, ladled the gruel at mealtime. He was assisted by one or two women.

The metal bowls never needed washing. The boys polished them with their spoons till they shone again, and when they had performed this operation (which never took very long, the spoons being nearly as large as the bowls), they would sit staring at the copper cauldron with eager eyes, as if they could have devoured the very metal of which it was composed.

Oliver Twisted and his companions suffered the tortures of slow starvation for a further six months. Oliver's thirteenth birthday came and went. Finally, a boy called Tiny Tim (who was extraordinarily tall for his age) got so ravenous and wild with hunger that one morning, as dawn broke, he attacked a smaller boy called Robbie and tried to eat him.

Robbie's screams alerted the others and Oliver, not pausing to worry about his own safety, tore Tim away and gripped the taller boy's arms fiercely.

Tim tried to break free, but Oliver would not be moved. His eyes grew hot and he could feel a strange heat flow down his arms and to his fingertips. The power felt angry and glorious. It was pure Rage and, as he held on to the other boy, Tim's struggles soon lessened. Oliver felt a stab of confusion go through him as he saw himself reflected in the gaze of the other boy and realised that his eyes were shining silver. *What's happening to me?*

Oliver let go of Tim, the mysterious power leaving him as quickly as it had come. He rubbed at his eyes, but the heat was gone. He found himself staring at Tim and gagged despite himself as he looked at the cannibal boy's face – it was covered with blood and something that looked very much like an ear was wedged in between the taller boy's lips.

Despite his onslaught being cut short, Tim closed his eyes in pleasure as he chewed down on the morsel, gobbling it up as if it was a rasher of bacon. He licked the corners of his mouth and sighed.

Oliver's eyes flitted over to Robbie. He was holding the side of his head – dark scarlet seeping through his pale fingers – and was warily watching the other boys who were eyeing up his remaining ear.

This has to stop, Oliver vowed to himself. *Before darkness takes hold of us all entirely.*

None too gently, Oliver pushed Tiny Tim to the floor. The lanky boy immediately rolled into a ball and began to cry as the full impact of what he had done sank in.

Oliver jumped on to his bunk. 'We can't let them win,' he called out, staring hard at the boys in his ward. 'We can't turn on each other, eat each other. If we do, we'll be the next to be sacrificed by the Brotherhood.'

A boy called Harry snorted. 'Pure thoughts will not fill our bellies, Twisted.' He looked at Robbie, who was still clutching at where his ear used to be. 'We need to eat. Maybe Tiny Tim had the right idea.'

There was a murmur of agreement from the other boys in the ward and Robbie's eyes widened as several took a step towards him.

'Wait!' Oliver demanded. 'Just wait. I'll get you more to eat. I promise.'

'How?' Harry demanded.

'I'll ask for more.' Oliver stood tall, back straight, and tried not to let the nervousness show on his face. 'Tonight I'll ask the cook for more.'

The evening arrived; the boys took their places. The cook, in his black and white uniform, stationed himself at the copper cauldron. His pauper assistants ranged themselves behind him and the gruel was served out. The gruel disappeared; the boys whispered to each other and nodded at Oliver, while his neighbours nudged him. Knowing that only by filling his companions' stomachs could he stop any more attacks, he rose from the table and, advancing to the cook, basin and spoon in hand, said:

'Please, sir, I want some more.'

The cook was a fat, healthy man, but he turned very pale. He gazed in stupefied astonishment at the small rebel for some seconds, and then clung on to the hot copper cauldron for support. He let out a bellow of pain as his hand sizzled on the hot metal. The smell of seared flesh filled the room. The cook's assistants were paralysed with wonder, the boys with fear.

'What?' said the cook at length, in a faint voice, cradling his burnt hand.

'Please, sir,' replied Oliver, 'I want some more.'

'The impudence!' The cook aimed a blow at Oliver's head with the ladle, but Oliver ducked, wrenched the utensil from the cook's hand and quickly spooned some gruel into his bowl.

His mouth instantly began to water as the steaming liquid hit the metal basin and for a moment all he wanted to do was bring it to his lips and gulp it down in one. But even as the gruel reached the very brim of the bowl and then slopped over the sides, Oliver knew he could not keep the food for himself; he had made a promise.

The stupefied cook's assistants finally leapt for Oliver, but he veered to his left and then sprang on to one of the long wooden tables. The assistants could not stop their momentum and crashed into each other, collapsing on the floor. As he raced to where his companions sat, the hands of the other children reached up at Oliver, begging for the bowl, others trying to wrestle it from his grip. 'There's more gruel left,' he shouted. 'Look in the cauldron. Take it! Take it, it's yours!'

Oliver's words had an extraordinary effect on the room. The starving boys rose from the benches, gripped their bowls and charged towards the cauldron. As the cook stared at the hungry tide of bodies, he shrieked aloud for the beadle and ran from the room. Oliver crouched low, put the bowl down in front of his companions and grinned. 'I told you I'd get you more.'

The Brotherhood of Fenris were sitting in solemn conclave when Mr Bumble rushed into the room.

Addressing the high priest, he said, 'Lord Skinim, I beg your pardon, sir! Oliver Twisted has attacked the cook to feed the other boys more gruel!'

There was a general start and a look of horror passed between the men at the table.

'*More gruel*!' said Lord Skinim. 'Compose yourself, Bumble, and answer me distinctly. Do I understand that Oliver took more gruel and gave it to others rather than eat it himself?'

'That boy needs to be hanged,' said the gentleman in the white waistcoat. 'He needs to be hanged before his good soul infects the others and we are left with none to sacrifice.'

'We cannot kill him,' said Lord Skinim heavily, from his high chair. 'I have seen the future in a dead child's glassy stare and the truth of Oliver Twisted has been revealed to me. He is a vessel of unrivalled power. A power poised on the edge of a blade. He can be used for supreme goodness or the most foul wickedness. No, my brothers, he cannot be killed, not until we can decide whether we can reveal and use his power for ourselves. He may well be the key to defeating the Knights of Nostradamus once and for all.'

An animated discussion took place. The beadle was ordered to take control of the dining room once more with the help of some of the Brotherhood. Oliver was put into instant confinement and the local undertaker, Mr Sowerberry, was brought before Lord Skinim.

They spoke long into the evening and so a deal was struck.

Chapter IV

Where Oliver goes to live with the undertaker and his wife

Oliver crouched in the corner of the windowless room. His throat felt raw from all his shouting, but he could no longer stand the sound of his cries which bounced straight off the walls of his prison. He spread his hands before his eyes to shut out the darkness and tried to take smaller breaths so that the air in the room might last him.

He started to tremble, drawing himself closer and closer to the wall, feeling even its cold, hard surface as protection in the gloom and loneliness which surrounded him.

There was the sound of a key in the lock and a shaft of light flooded over him. Mr Bumble stood in the doorway. The beadle threw a clean shirt at Oliver and ordered him to put it on. To Oliver's astonishment, Mr

Bumble then brought him, with his own hands, a basin of gruel and some bread.

At this sight, Oliver began to shake again, even though he hated himself for doing it. He thought, not unnaturally, that the Brotherhood of Fenris must have determined to kill him for some useful purpose or they never would have begun to fatten him up in this way.

'Don't make your eyes red, Oliver, but eat your food and be thankful,' said Mr Bumble, in a tone of impressive pomposity. 'You're a-going to be made an apprentice.'

'An apprentice, sir!' said Oliver.

'Yes,' replied Mr Bumble. 'The Brotherhood of Fenris can't risk having you in the workhouse, stirring up goodness and decency. They are a-going to apprentice you – set you up in life and make a man out of you, a man in their image.'

As Mr Bumble paused to take breath, after delivering this address in a bombastic voice, Oliver very calmly said: 'I will never be like them.' His skinny fingers clenched into fists. 'There was a time when this world was good – before hell's mouth was opened – I heard Mrs Mann's maid say. I will live as if that better world still exists.'

The beadle snorted with laughter. 'What is done cannot be undone. That door was opened and cannot be closed. Come,' said Mr Bumble brusquely. 'It is time to meet your new master!'

Mr Sowerberry was a tall, gaunt, large-jointed man, attired in a suit of threadbare black, with darned cotton stockings of the same colour and shoes to answer. Being in the business of funerals, his features were not naturally intended to wear a smile.

'I have taken the measure of the two boys that were sacrificed last night, Mr Bumble,' said the undertaker as he spied the beadle outside the gates of the workhouse.

'You'll make your fortune, Mr Sowerberry,' said Mr Bumble, tapping the man on the shoulder with his cane.

'Think so?' asked the undertaker in a tone which half admitted and half disputed the probability of the event. 'The prices allowed by the Brotherhood of Fenris are very small, Mr Bumble.'

'So are the coffins,' replied the beadle with a laugh.

Mr Sowerberry was much tickled at this and chuckled a long time. 'True, true, Mr Bumble,' he said at length. 'There's no denying that since the new system of starving has come in, the coffins are somewhat narrower and more shallow than they used to be, but we must have some profit, Mr Bumble. Well-seasoned timber is expensive, sir; and all the iron handles come, by canal, from Birmingham.'

'Well, well,' said Mr Bumble. 'Every trade has its

drawbacks. A fair profit for sound business is, of course, allowable.' The beadle thrust Oliver in front of him. 'Talking of business, here is the boy.'

'Aha!' said the undertaker, looking Oliver up and down. 'Let us take him back to the funeral home. Mrs Sowerberry will want to see him.'

They walked in silence along the dusty, country path. Oliver wondered for a moment if he might be able to run away, but the weight of the beadle's hand on his shoulder told him that such an idea was sheer fancy.

The undertaker's wife, who had just put up the shutters of the shop, was making some entries in her daybook by the light of a dismal candle when Mr Bumble, Mr Sowerberry and Oliver entered.

'Oh! That's the boy, is it?' said Mrs Sowerberry, raising the candle above her head, to get a better view of Oliver. 'The boy that the Brotherhood want us to turn wicked.'

In the candlelight, Oliver could see that the undertaker's wife was a squeezed-up woman, with a sly face.

'Dear me!' she continued. 'He's very small.'

'Why, he *is* rather small.' Bumble looked at Oliver as if it were the boy's fault that he was no bigger. 'He is small. There's no denying it. But he'll grow, Mrs Sowerberry, he'll grow.'

'Ah! I dare say he will,' replied the lady with a twisted

smile. 'On an undertaker's diet, he'll develop well enough. Get downstairs, little bag o' bones.' With this, the undertaker's wife opened a side door and pushed Oliver down a steep flight of stairs into a stone cell, damp and dark. In it sat a grubby-looking girl, in shoes down at heel and blue stockings very much out of repair.

'Here, Charlotte,' said Mr Sowerberry, who had followed Oliver down. 'Give this boy some dinner.'

A plateful of slosh was set before Oliver. Looking closer, he could make out ropes of intestines, the ripple of stomach tissue and grey slivers of brain. The gloopy mush bubbled and gurgled and an eyeball proudly floated to the top.

'You isn't too dainty to eat it, are you, boy? You ain't too good or too pure?'

Mr Sowerberry laughed. He plunged his hand into the mushy guts and held it out under Oliver's nose. 'Eat. We waste nothing here at the embalmer's shop – it's an undertaker's privilege to have a constant supply of meat.'

Oliver shook his head. 'Haven't you heard? You are what you eat.' He curled his lip as he looked at the undertaker. 'Explains a lot.'

Mr Sowerberry scowled. 'A jester, are you? A clown?' He thrust the glistening innards further forwards.

Oliver backed away, but Mr Bumble, Mrs Sowerberry and the girl Charlotte were suddenly behind him, pushing him towards the undertaker. He clamped his lips shut as Mr Sowerberry tried to thrust the guts into his mouth. The warm and wet gore covered his face, tickling the inside of his nose, moistening the end of his lashes.

'Taste it, boy,' the undertaker snarled, grinding the gristle harder into his face, but Oliver pressed his lips together even more tightly.

A tide of black swelled up behind the orphan's eyes and pain lashed round his chest as his air ran out. Oliver's knees buckled beneath him. The last thing he saw as he crashed to the ground was the bowl of guts smashing down beside him and a rheumy eyeball rolling across the flagstone floor.

Chapter V

In which Oliver has a most informative
talk with a corpse

Oliver awoke to find himself in a coffin and
wondered for a moment if he might be dead, and
if so, why was he blinking in the darkness?

With a feeling of dread, which many people a good
deal older than he will be at no loss to understand, he
placed his hand against the rough wood of the lid and
pushed. He breathed a sigh of relief as it shifted aside
without too much pressure.

Oliver slowly sat up, wiping at the blood that still
caked his mouth. He was not surprised to find himself
in the undertaker's workroom. A small lamp had been
placed on a nearby bench and illuminated the chamber.
He climbed out of the coffin and tried the heavy wooden
door, but it was locked.

Against the wall were arranged a long row of elm

boards cut in the same shape, looking in the dim light like high-shouldered ghosts with their hands in their breeches pockets.

Coffin-plates, elm-chips, bright-headed nails and shreds of black cloth lay scattered on the floor. On the wall behind the counter was a painting of two burly death lictors, with heavy whips round their necks. They stood in front of a horse-drawn hearse, ready to fight off the grave-robbing ghouls who crept towards them.

The shop was stuffy and hot. The atmosphere seemed tainted with the smell of decay.

A glossy black coffin on trestles, which stood in the middle of the shop, looked so gloomy and death-like that a cold tremble came over Oliver despite the warmth of the room.

There was a creak followed by a shuffling sound, and then a crash as the black coffin's lid was thrown back and on to the floor. A frightful form slowly reared its head and Oliver's mouth gaped like a wound. Fear pressed heavily on his shoulders and he could not move as he stared at the animated corpse. *Surely it is a woe-begotten, come to tear me apart*, Oliver thought, remembering all that Mrs Mann had said of the creatures in her bedtime stories.

The male cadaver turned to face Oliver and tried to speak, but found that its lips had been sewn shut. The corpse's sunken eyes rolled furiously in their sockets and it tore at the threads with clawed hands, working its jaw open until all the stitches had been pulled apart.

'Please,' Oliver begged. 'Please don't devour me.'

The corpse's grey-clay face broke into a smile. 'I have no intention of devouring you. I am not a woe-begotten – how very amusing. I have a message for you, young Oliver, but I must be quick. My spirit cannot stay long in this broken body.'

'A message,' Oliver repeated in bemusement. 'From whom?'

'Your mother,' the cadaver replied. 'I'm told she was a white witch when she lived and still has some of her magic even though she's passed on. You must go to London, Oliver, that is where your destiny awaits. You have power, boy; you will be humanity's salvation or damnation.'

'My mother?' Oliver said the words, but they felt like they belonged to another language. 'Who was she? Where does she want me to go in London? Where will I live?'

'No lad of spirit need want in London,' the corpse replied. 'There are many ways to live in that vast city. Your mother was an extraordinary woman, and the daughter of a powerful man called –'

There was a turn of the key in the door and the

40

cadaver collapsed back in its coffin like a scarecrow slipping off its pole.

A sour-faced young man stood in the doorway. 'Mr Sowerberry wants to know what all the commotion is. Some of us are trying to sleep.'

Oliver bowed his head. 'I didn't know where I was when I woke up. I knocked one of the coffins off its trestles by accident.'

The young man wrinkled his nose in distaste. 'So yer the new boy?'

'Yes,' replied Oliver, his mind still whirling with what the corpse had said, or had he imagined the whole thing?

'How old are yer?' enquired the sour-faced boy.

'Thirteen,' replied Oliver, his eyes finally focusing properly on the figure in front of him.

A smirk crossed the boy's face. 'Then I'm three years older and I'll whop yer if I choose to.'

Oliver had met his fair share of bullies in his life and thought that this one – with his large head, red nose and small eyes – looked like the biggest and dumbest of them all. He chose to say nothing in reply and instead looked over the boy's shoulder, wondering whether he could make a run for it.

The boy suddenly looked monstrously fierce and said that Oliver had best keep his eyes fixed on him, if he knew what was good for him.

'Yer don't know who I am, I suppose, bag o' bones,' continued the older boy, taking a lumbering step forward.

'No, I do not,' rejoined Oliver.

'I'm Mister Noah Claypole,' said the older boy, 'and you're under me, so shut up and go back to sleep.' With that, Mr Claypole administered a kick to Oliver, slammed the door shut behind him and locked it.

Oliver crept over to the glossy coffin, where only moments before the dead body had spoken to him. Looking down, he could see the ripped threads that had once sealed the cadaver's mouth. 'It was not a fanciful notion then,' Oliver whispered into the quiet room. 'This corpse did speak to me.' He shook the cadaver's shoulder as if he could reawaken it, but the dead man was as stiff as a plank of wood and his skin cold to touch. Oliver stood there for what felt like an age, but the cadaver did not stir again.

A dismal feeling swamped Oliver. He was alone in a strange place, and we all know how chilled and desolate the best of us will sometimes feel in such a situation. He had no friends to care for, or to care for him. The absence of any remembrance of a mother's loved and well-remembered face sank heavily into his heart.

Yet a spark of something suddenly lit within the boy. *I may not remember her, but I am not forgotten by my mother*, he thought to himself. *She sent me a message and I will heed it. I will go to London, as soon as I can get away from this place.*

Oliver crept back into the coffin which was his narrow bed and closed his eyes. In his dreams, he imagined a long, winding path and tall grass waving gently on steep banks. The sound of old deep bells rang with each step that he took towards his destiny . . .

Oliver had been prisoner at the undertaker's some three weeks or a month. He built coffins, stitched lips and dug graves. But not once did he allow the undertakers to feed him their foul food, and nothing Mr Sowerberry tried could turn Oliver to evil.

But one night, Mr Sowerberry had a rather fine idea. The undertaker shared it with his wife, while having dinner with her in the back parlour.

'My dear, I want to ask your advice,' he said.

After a short duration, the permission was most graciously given.

'It's only about young Twisted, my dear,' said Mr Sowerberry. 'A very good-looking boy, that, my dear.'

'He would be if he ate the meat we tried to give him, instead of nibbling at nothing but bread. He just gets thinner and thinner.'

'There's an expression of melancholy in his face, my dear,' resumed Mr Sowerberry, 'which is very interesting.

43

He would make a delightful mute, my love. Our customers would surely appreciate his silent glumness as he helped to bury their loved ones.'

Mrs Sowerberry looked up with an expression of considerable wonderment and excitement. 'But what would the Brotherhood say?' she asked. 'They sent him to us to make him evil, or at least a little bit wicked.'

'They didn't say anything about him keeping his tongue,' Mr Sowerberry responded confidently. 'Besides, we are not doing a very good job of turning the boy. He is as good now as he was a month ago and we have still seen no sign of these supposed powers that Lord Skinim told me he has.'

Mrs Sowerberry frowned, and then, with much sharpness, asked why such an obvious suggestion had not presented itself to her husband's mind before. 'Taking his tongue and indulging in other tortures is bound to provoke a reaction,' she mused.

Mr Sowerberry rightly guessed that this was an agreement. It was speedily determined, therefore, that Oliver would be tied down and his tongue removed as soon as the correct tools could be fetched.

The occasion was not long in coming. Half an hour after breakfast the next morning, Mrs Sowerberry arrived home from the blacksmith, with roses in her cheeks, and drew forth a large pair of locking pliers which she handed over to Mr Sowerberry.

'Aha!' said the undertaker, glancing over them with a lively countenance. 'This will do just the job.'

There was a knock on the door and Mr Bumble entered the shop. Supporting his cane against the counter, he reached into his pocket, took out his pixie-skinned wallet and from it selected a small scrap of paper which he handed over to Mr Sowerberry.

'An order for a coffin, eh?' Mr Sowerberry said, trying to hide his disappointment at the interruption to his planned entertainment. He slid the locking pliers beneath the counter.

'Aye, and it is urgent. It is for one of the Brotherhood. Fenris discovered that he was praying to his rival, his banished son Sköll, and so a wolf came in the night. We've managed to scrape up most of the pieces and a rather sodden white waistcoat.'

Mrs Sowerberry scowled. 'I guess we will have to wait to complete our business then, husband?'

The undertaker nodded.

'You'll be kept busy all day, I'd imagine,' explained Mr Bumble. 'We'll need the coffin first and a funeral pyre afterwards.' The beadle fastened the strap of the wallet which, like himself, was very corpulent.

'I best be getting on then.' The undertaker disappeared into his workshop and Mr Bumble left the shop.

'Humph!' was all Mrs Sowerberry had to say as she plonked herself down behind the counter and opened her daybook. She found some comfort though in the adage, 'Good things come to those that wait.' Her fingers lightly touched the locking pliers and she smiled.

'Come near the fire, Noah,' said Charlotte, below stairs, later that morning. 'I saved a nice little bit of liver for you from master's breakfast. Oliver, shut that door at Mister Noah's back and take them crusts that I've put out on the cover of the bread-pan. Make haste, for they'll want you to mind the shop. D'ye hear?'

'D'ye hear, bag o' bones?' said Noah Claypole.

'Lor, Noah!' said Charlotte. 'Let the boy alone. He's got enough to think about. Have you heard what the master and missis want to do to his tongue?' She made a cutting movement with her hand. 'Snip, snip.'

Noah ignored her. 'Let him alone!' he said. 'Why everybody lets him alone enough. Neither his father nor his mother will ever interfere with him. None of his relations have ever claimed him. It's just little ole bag o' bones, all by himself. Eh, Charlotte?'

'Oh, you mean soul!' said Charlotte, bursting into a hearty laugh, in which she was joined by Noah; after which they both looked scornfully at Oliver Twisted.

Oliver chewed on his stale bit of bread, thinking only

of what the corpse had said all those weeks ago and how he might get to London. Not even Charlotte's comment about the fate of his tongue had pierced his reverie.

Intent upon tormenting Oliver further, Noah pulled Oliver's hair and twitched his ears. He then expressed his opinion that he was a 'freak' and that he couldn't wait to see the day that the Brotherhood sacrificed him. When this still got no reaction, Noah did what many sometimes do to this day, when they wish to wound. He became rather personal in his remarks.

'Bag o' bones,' said Noah. 'How's your mother?'

'She's dead,' replied Oliver, goaded out of his musings at last. 'Don't you say anything about her to me!'

Oliver's colour rose as he said this. His breathing quickened and there was a curious working of the mouth and nostrils, which Mr Claypole thought must be the immediate precursor of a violent fit of crying. Under this impression he returned to the charge.

'What did she die of, bag o' bones?' said Noah.

'Of a broken heart, some of our old nurses told me,' replied Oliver, more as if he were talking to himself than answering Noah. 'I think I know what it must be to die of that.'

'Who's broken your heart then?' asked Noah.

'Not *you*,' replied Oliver, sharply. 'Nothing you can say can hurt so you'd better not say anything more to me about my mother; you'd better not!'

'Better not!' exclaimed Noah. 'Better not! Don't be impudent. *Your* mother, she was a nice 'un she was. Oh lor!' And here, Noah nodded his head expressively and curled up as much of his small red nose as muscular action could collect together.

'Yer know, bag o' bones,' continued Noah, emboldened by Oliver's silence and speaking in a jeering tone of affected pity. 'It can't be helped now, and of course yer couldn't help it then, but yer must know, yer mother was a regular right-down bad 'un. A foul, stinking witch I'd bet.'

'What did you say?' enquired Oliver, looking up very quickly.

'A foul, stinking witch,' replied Noah coolly. 'And it's a great deal better that she died when she did, or else she'd have been causing all kinds of trouble I'm sure.'

Crimson with fury, Oliver started up and he felt Rage course through him. A bolt of fire left his fingers and the chair and table in front of him exploded in a shower of sparks and ash. Oliver seized Noah by the throat, shook him in the violence of his Rage till the other boy's teeth chattered in his head and, collecting his whole force into one heavy blow, felled him to the ground.

Oliver's blood felt like it was on fire. His fingers were still warm from where the flame had sprung from their tips. His chest heaved, his shoulders and spine were as straight as a board, his eyes silver and vivid. His whole person changed as he stood glaring over the cowardly tormentor who now lay crouching at his feet. He was filled with the power he had experienced only once before when he stopped Tiny Tim back at the workhouse. He felt strong enough to take Noah's skull in his hand and crush it as easily as chalk.

'He'll murder me!' blubbered Noah. 'Charlotte! Missis! Here's the new boy a-murdering of me! He made the table explode. Help! Help! Oliver's gone mad! Look at his eyes, Char – lotte!'

Noah's shouts were responded to by a loud scream from Charlotte who was hiding behind the upturned table. And an even louder scream from Mrs Sowerberry who had paused on the staircase till she was quite certain that it was consistent with the preservation of human life to come further down.

'Oh, you little wretch!' screamed Charlotte, seizing Oliver's leg with her utmost force, which was about equal to that of a moderately strong man of particularly good constitution.

Oliver kicked away her grasp and ran to the foot of the stairs. The blood was still pounding in his head and his cheeks were aflame. He glared at Mrs Sowerberry. 'Get out of my way,' he said. 'I do not want to hurt you.'

Mrs Sowerberry smiled. 'Little bag o' bones has found his spirit and, by the looks of it, power as well. Lord Skinim was right about you, Oliver. You have,' she paused and stared into his silver eyes, '*potential*.' The undertaker's wife stood to one side. 'Run, little Oliver, run away, but the Brotherhood will find you.'

Oliver suddenly felt as weak as a kitten as he looked at the certainty in Mrs Sowerberry's sly gaze. His strange strength had now deserted him, but not his bravery. Thrusting back his shoulders, he pushed past Mrs Sowerberry and thundered up the stairs. Taking a deep breath, he pulled open the shop door and spilt out into the morning sunlight.

Chapter VI

Where Noah Claypole delivers some very bad news to Mr Bumble

Noah Claypole ran along the streets at his swiftest pace and paused not once for breath until he reached the workhouse gate. Resting for a moment to collect a good burst of sobs and an imposing show of tears and terror, he banged loudly on the metal bars.

An old lady opened the door and looked out suspiciously at him. 'What do you want,' she snarled. 'Hope you are not here to sell off any of your kin. The Brotherhood is not in need of any new children. They –'

'Mr Bumble! Mr Bumble!' cried Noah, 'I need to speak to him, now.'

There was the sound of heavy footsteps on the creaky oaken floor. 'What is all the fuss?' asked Mr Bumble, with a glint of annoyance in his piggy eyes.

'It's Oliver,' Noah said.

'What about Oliver?' Bumble said, stepping out of the door. He shooed the old lady away.

'Oh, Mr Bumble, sir!' said Noah. 'He's run away, sir. But it weren't our fault. He turned vicious.'

Noah wrung his hands so hard his knuckles clicked. 'He tried to murder me, sir; and then he tried to murder Charlotte, and then the missis. Oh! What dreadful pain I'm in. There was fire at his fingertips, silver in his eyes. I saw it.' Noah began to writhe and twist his body into an extensive variety of eel-like positions to show Mr Bumble just how much agony he was in.

'Quit your worming and squirming,' Mr Bumble snapped. 'We've to get Oliver back before the Brotherhood find out.'

'Too late for that, Bumble,' a deep voice said from behind him. Out of the shadows of the workhouse, Lord Skinim, the high priest of the Brotherhood, emerged. Mr Bumble took a hasty step back and collided with Noah, who gave a yelp of pain as Mr Bumble's heavy foot crushed his much smaller one.

The high priest loomed on the step. His skin was as grey as ash and he stood blinking in the sun as if he was not used to the light.

'Oliver needs to be found, Bumble,' the high priest

rasped. 'That boy is the key to defeating the Knights of Nostradamus.' He licked his lips, a wet slash of crimson in a grey wasteland. 'With young Oliver as our puppet, our enemies will not be able to challenge our final dominion. But if he falls into the wrong hands . . .' The high priest paused and reached out with long, tapering fingers to grasp Mr Bumble's shoulder, and squeezed. 'Well, suffice it to say, Bumble, that there would be grave consequences. Grave consequences for all of us.'

Mr Bumble tried not to whimper as he felt Lord Skinim's long nails pierce his clothes and cut into the flesh beneath. 'We'll get him back, sir,' he babbled. 'Won't we, Noah?'

'Yes, sir, we'll find him,' Noah whined like a kicked dog.

The high priest released Mr Bumble's shoulder. 'No, I will locate Oliver with a scrying spell and send an associate to collect him. Someone not as incompetent as yourselves.' Lord Skinim looked thoughtful. 'But I have another job for you. Bring me the Sowerberrys.' The high priest smiled, showing his tomb-like teeth. 'I gave them something precious to look after and they were careless with it.' His lips turned downwards. 'There must and will always be a reckoning. Run along now and get them.'

'Yes, sir.' Noah Claypole turned tail and took himself off with all speed to the undertaker's shop.

Mr Bumble adjusted his hat, grabbed his cane and ran after the lad.

Chapter VII

In which Oliver encounters a strange young gentleman on the road to London, and other things besides

With the Sowerberry's house left far behind him, Oliver stopped running and took in his bearings. He had taken the route he remembered seeing the waggons tread as they went toiling up the hill and out towards the city. He now stood on a footpath that stretched across the fields and which, after some distance, would lead out again to the road to London.

Oliver could not believe that the Sowerberrys would care enough to come after him but he decided to avoid the main roads as much as possible. He struck out on the path, passing barren fields, realising that this was the same footpath he had walked with Mr Bumble when he was first taken from the bloodfarm to the workhouse.

Oliver felt an unexpected pang of affection for his old home. The farm had been a cradle of horrors, and Mrs

Mann a cruel mistress, but he had understood her and what each day would bring. Now here he was, on his way to London, because a corpse told him to.

'No, because I have a destiny,' Oliver corrected himself. He scratched at his tangled hair, feeling the crawl of lice beneath his fingertips. 'Or I was delusional with hunger and imagined it all,' he muttered.

Oliver reached the stile where the footpath terminated and once more led to the high road. He kept to the hedgerows, dipping out of sight at the sound of any approach. As he hid behind the hedges, thorns digging into his coarse shirt and cold seeping through his worn shoes, he began cursing himself for his caution. Yet Oliver couldn't shake off the feeling that he was being pursued.

He trudged on and had diminished the distance between himself and London by a full four miles more before the tight fist of hunger squeezed his stomach, forcing him to sit by a milestone on the roadside.

Oliver's gaze fixed on the engraved stone. He could not read all the words but he recognised the number 65 and the word LONDON.

'Sixty-five miles to go,' Oliver groaned. Despair crept upon him. How was he going to walk that far with no food and no money to buy any? He looked down the long road. 'And what will I do when I get there?'

A slight breeze tickled the hairs on the back of his neck and it almost felt like a mother's touch on his nape. Oliver felt strangely comforted.

'It's not so bad,' he told the empty air. 'London is such a big place. Nobody, not even the Brotherhood, can find me there!'

Oliver was suddenly reminded of what the corpse had said. 'No lad of spirit need want in London.' He thought of the Rage that had burnt through his veins when he had stood up to Noah and the Sowerberrys, the power he had felt flame at his fingertips. He thought of his mother and the magic that she must have had if she was a white witch.

'I have spirit,' Oliver murmured. 'And if my mother wants me to go to London, then that is where I will go.' He jumped to his feet and strode forward once more.

Oliver walked twenty miles that day and all that time tasted nothing but a stale crust of bread and a few draughts of water, which he begged at cottage doors by the roadside. He lay down in a ditch that night and counted the stars, willing himself to sleep and ignore the rumbling in his stomach.

He felt cold and stiff when he woke up next morning, and so hungry that he ate withered blades of grass by the roadside and drank from a muddy hoofprint in the road.

He had walked no more than twelve miles when night closed in again. His feet were sore and his legs so weak that they trembled beneath him.

Another night passed in the bleak, damp air and when he set forward on his journey the next morning, he could hardly crawl along.

Oliver was not educated. Indeed, he could not even write his name, but he was not stupid and knew that he couldn't go on much longer on foot. So despite the risk of being seen by one of the Brotherhood's agents, he waited at the bottom of a steep hill for a stagecoach to come down, so he could try to beg passage.

After five coaches bowled past him without taking any notice, Oliver took desperate action. As he heard the roll of the stagecoach, he stepped into the road and spread his arms wide.

The coach thundered towards him, and Oliver's eyes widened as he saw that the carriage was drawn not by horses but rather four massive creatures with legs like tree trunks and hides that were grey and leathery. A long horn protruded from each beast's snout.

Oliver swallowed hard, but held his position. The coach came to a juddering stop. The driver on top of the carriage began to curse at him in a language he didn't understand and a lady with a nose as sharp and straight as a blade stuck her head out of the window. 'What do you think you're doing?' she demanded.

Oliver took a step towards her.

'No, no, stay there,' the woman screeched, 'or I will get my driver to release the Emela-ntouka on you.'

'The Emela what?' Oliver asked.

'The Emela-ntouka.' The woman gestured to the massive creatures pulling the carriage. 'They are all the way from Timbuktu and they weren't cheap, let me tell you, but they are fierce if roused and will fight to the death to protect their owners.' She pursed her lips. 'They are exactly what are needed during these dark, dark times.'

'They are indeed dark times, my lady,' Oliver said holding on to her words like a drowning person. 'I need to get to London. Could you please let me ride with you? I would forever be in your debt.'

'I should think not,' the woman snorted. 'You could be anything. A shapeshifter ready to rob me blind, or even a vengeful ghost.' She sniffed. 'You look pale enough.'

'I am just a boy,' Oliver said.

A boy who speaks to the dead, his conscience whispered inside. *A boy with Rage and fire in his hands. No, not really like other boys.*

'I do not care who or what you are,' the woman said. 'But I suggest you keep on walking. It is not safe to stand still on the road. You may get leapt upon.'

She thumped her cane on the roof of the carriage. 'Drive on,' she hollered. 'And run him down if he does not move.'

Oliver jumped out of the way as the carriage charged past him, leaving as its gift a cloud of dust for him to choke on. His shoulders sagged and he did the only thing he could: he kept on walking. He only stopped once to rip the sleeves off his shirt and wrap them round his feet, which were a mass of blisters and bloody, scabbed skin. His shoes were completely worn through, the soles riddled with holes. He left them on the side of the road and pressed on.

Days passed and Oliver finally came to a village on the outskirts of London. Everywhere he looked he could see large painted boards fixed to the walls, but Mrs Mann had never been bothered enough to teach any of the orphans to read and so he had no idea what they said.

He tried to beg for some bread at a farmer's house, but was told to move away from the door before they set the dogs on him. Every house he knocked on was the same. No one would even open the door to speak to him. The streets were empty and the shops boarded-up.

That evening, Oliver picked lice out of his hair and swallowed them whole, tears of disgust seeping from his eyes as he felt the tickle of legs at the back of his throat. When the night came, he turned into a field and, creeping close under a cone-shaped hayrick, settled down to sleep.

He was awoken by the wind that moaned dismally over the empty fields. A low, persistent moan that would not stop. The cold had seeped deep into Oliver's bones and made him shiver so vigorously that he thought his teeth might crack from all the chattering.

The gale's moan was even fiercer now, and so loud that it felt like the wind was right on top of him. His house of hay began to rock back and forth, stalks of straw falling in a spiky shower. Fear scraped along Oliver's spine for beneath the moan of the wind he could hear grunts and growls of exertion. This was no wind – someone was trying to lift the hayrick off him.

Oliver clenched his fists. 'I'm not going back,' he screamed over and over again. 'I'm not going back.'

The moaning stopped for a moment and then so did the grunts. All that could be heard was the creak of the hay cone as it slowly toppled to one side and crashed to the ground.

A cloudless sky allowed the full moon to illuminate him and Oliver felt like a snail that had been ripped out of its shell. He got shakily to his feet, ready to face his pursuer, protests hot in his mouth.

But the words disintegrated on Oliver's tongue

because it was not a member of the Brotherhood who stared at him, with the promise of death in his yellow eyes. It was not Mr Sowerberry's face that was riddled with gaping holes where maggots frothed. It was not Mr Bumble who stank of decay and was so stick-thin that his skin hung like rags from his body.

'FLESH,' groaned the creature in front of him.

'Woe-begotten,' Oliver whispered back.

'FLESH.' The woe-begotten bared his teeth, which were ragged and black.

'FLESH.' Another moan came from behind and Oliver turned to see two more woe-begottens. They began to shuffle towards him, barefoot – toes blue from cold, arms outstretched.

Oliver ducked under their grasp and sprinted to his left, tearing across the field. The woe-begottens cried out in fury at losing their prey and their shuffling lope soon turned into an awkward, stumbling run.

Oliver was faster than them, but he knew a woe-begotten never gave up once it had the scent of you in its nose. They could run forever. Oliver grimaced and wished that he didn't know that fact. But Mrs Mann had been a keen storyteller and her favourite tales were always about woe-begottens and their hunting packs.

'Once you're bitten, you will turn,' she had told the orphans. 'Once those teeth sink in deep, you will become just as ravenous for flesh as the demon who made the very first woe-begotten.'

Oliver had been walking for seven days. His legs felt weak and his breath was a rolled up ball of pain in his chest.

I cannot run forever, Oliver thought. *But I have the Rage. I can crush their skulls, rip their heads from their shoulders. I could send a bolt of fire through their hearts.*

He stopped, scrunched up his eyes and waited for that wave of strange strength to course through him. He waited for the tingle. He waited for the burn at his fingertips. But nothing happened.

The slap of bare feet behind him on the wet grass was getting louder, the moan of the woe-begottens rose as one song, their hissing call for flesh ripping the air.

Oliver clenched his fists and tried again, searching inside himself for the Rage, but still nothing. The panting breath of the woe-begottens was right behind him now and he could almost feel their cool breath on his neck, imagine their claw-like hands reaching for him.

'What are you doin', you bloody idiot?' a voice called from across the fallow field. 'Run!'

Oliver's eyes snapped open and he spotted a boy wearing a top hat gesturing at him wildly from a perched position up on the fence.

'Come on, stop gawping and start running,' the boy hollered, starting to wave his top hat in the air.

Oliver dipped his head and charged forward, his legs and arms pumping like pistons on a steam train. The woe-begottens howled with fury at his sudden acceleration and as he looked over his shoulder he could see their jerky gait increase speed.

Blood and pus ran between Oliver's toes, soaking the strips that bound his feet as he pounded across the ground, but he did not falter. He reached the fence and the boy in the top hat gripped his hand and hauled him over. They stood together, studying each other in the moonlight.

The other boy was about his own age, but was like no one that Oliver had ever seen before. His skin was a deep, polished mahogany and he had long-lashed, treacly-coloured eyes and full lips that that stretched into a smile.

The boy looked short for his age, with rather bow legs. His hat was stuck on the top of his head so lightly that it threatened to fall off at every moment. He was adorned with two lengths of filthy string round his neck and from each piece a key dangled. He wore a man's coat, which reached nearly to his heels, and he had turned the cuffs back halfway up his arms, to get his hands out of the sleeves, apparently with the ultimate view of ramming them into the pockets of his corduroy trousers. He was altogether as roistering and swaggering a young gentleman as ever stood five feet two, or something less.

'I'm the dodger,' the boy said, thrusting out a grubby hand. 'But everyone calls me Dodge.'

'I'm Oliver Twisted,' Oliver said.

'Nice to meet you, Olly mate.' Dodge's eyes glanced over Oliver's shoulder and he yanked his top hat further down on his head. 'Now, if you're quite finished dawdling, I think it's time we got out of here.' He sniffed. 'Unless you want to be ripped apart by a woe-begotten?'

Chapter VIII

Where Oliver digs up a dead body

'W here are we going?' Oliver asked, trying to keep up with Dodge's quick strides as they crossed another field.

'The graveyard, over Barnet way.'

'And why are we going there?' Oliver asked.

Dodge stopped and looked at Oliver, his dark brown eyes wide with incredulity. 'My, my, how green are you? We are going to the graveyard because we have a pack of woe-begottens on our tail. You do want to get rid of them, don't you?'

'Yes, of course,' Oliver said. He could feel his cheeks warming. He didn't like the idea of being green. He liked even less the fact that he didn't know why going to the graveyard was going to rid them of the woe-begottens.

Dodge rolled his eyes, but clearly took pity on him.

'Decay, mate. The reek of rotten flesh and the stench of what festers will save our skins.' He began to walk quickly once again. 'Right now, the woe-begottens' noses are filled with our scent. The smell of our fresh, living flesh intoxicates them. They will not stop until they take a bite out of us and change us. They will follow us to the end of our days.' Dodge adjusted his hat. 'Woe-begottens do not sleep, and they do not tire once they have fixed on their prey.' He grinned. 'But if we can get to the graveyard, we will be able to remedy that, throw them off the scent so to speak.'

Oliver nodded. The overwhelming stench of dead bodies he understood – the undertaker's house had stunk of it. No amount of scrubbing had ever seemed to get the smell out of his skin.

The moan of the woe-begottens' cry echoed behind them, but Oliver and Dodge ran on, not pausing once to look back.

They soon arrived at the wrought-iron gate of the graveyard, but found it to be bolted shut. The gate towered above them and an ornate, swirling mass of metal ivy leaves curled round the rails as if they would strangle the rods of iron. Spears of metal lined the top of the gate and glinted in the moonlight.

'Right, we better get climbing,' Oliver said, grabbing the slippery black rails. He placed one foot on a curling metal vine and tried to haul himself upwards. With a wet, slurping sound, he immediately slipped back down. Oliver thrust his shoulders back and tried again, but only succeeded in landing in a heap at the bottom of the gate, sharp bits of gravel cutting into his backside.

The dodger let out a bark of laughter and doubled over as mirth shook his body. 'Nice work, Olly!'

'Well, you climb it then,' Oliver snapped.

Dodge snorted. 'How in hell's mouth do you suppose we climb that gate? And even if we did, how would we get over those spiky things?' He rubbed absently at one of the keys that hung from his neck. 'I could do myself an injury.'

The moan of the woe-begottens ripped through the air once again.

Oliver glared at Dodge. 'Why did you bring us here if we can't get in?' he asked.

'Who said we can't get in?' The dodger held out his hand to Oliver, who looked puzzled. 'Well, go on, take it. I won't bite.'

Oliver gripped the other boy's palm.

'Whatever happens, don't let go, all right?' Dodge said.

The boy began to blink rapidly and then, with a rasp of breath, the dodger's body started to shift and twist, soon becoming as wispy and insubstantial as smoke. Oliver stiffened as he felt his own arm begin to tingle and, looking down, he saw that it had begun to fade and turn into smoke as well. He tried to yank his arm back, but a voice stopped him.

'Don't let go.' Dodge's voice was coming out of a column of smoke that drifted beside Oliver. 'And don't stare, Olly, you need to concentrate. Let yourself become smoke and then follow me through the rails.'

Oliver swallowed hard as he felt the smoke cover his chest and climb up his throat. Looking down, he could no longer see his body, just black cloud, and he suddenly felt light, without pain or concern. He drifted forward as Dodge tugged at him, feeling the cold of the metal squeeze him as he slipped through the rails and into the graveyard.

Oliver's sense of peace gave way to hunger for even more freedom and it gnawed deep in his gut. He wanted to float higher, climb into the air and spread himself across the sky. He soared upwards, but found himself yanked down to earth.

'Enough of that, Olly,' Dodge said reproachfully. 'Time to turn back.'

'No wai –' Oliver's plea was cut off by a sharp pain as he felt bone knit back together, flesh crawl over limbs, even the roughness of clothes on his skin. The pain of his bloodied and blistered feet came back to him worse than ever.

His hand was still in Dodge's and he snatched it back. 'How did you do that?' he demanded. *Why did you turn me back?* his thoughts whispered pitifully.

'I turned us into smoke and got us into the graveyard,' Dodge replied. 'It's what I do. That's why people call me the dodger.'

There was a clattering sound on the other side of the gate and Oliver turned to see the pack of woe-begottens running at the metal railings. They squealed like stuck pigs as they rebounded off the jagged metal, bloody gashes from the gate slashed into their skin.

Dodge snorted. 'Woe-begottens are so predictably stupid, but they will eventually work out a way to get in. Come on, we've got to move.'

Dodge dashed off and Oliver followed close behind. 'But we'll be all right now, won't we?' Oliver asked. 'They won't be able to smell us now we are in here with all these dead bodies.'

'Green doesn't even begin to cover it, does it?' Dodge crowed as they made their way over the ground as fast as they could. 'Being in a graveyard is not enough, Olly. We can't just have a whiff of death around us. It's got to get deep in our skin till our pores are clogged with it.'

'How are we going to do that?' Oliver's frustration made his voice rough. 'And when are you going to tell me how you turned us into smoke?'

The dodger grinned. 'No need to sound so vexed, Olly! I've got no secrets. My grandmother taught me how to do the smoke thing. I just can't hold it for very long.' Dodge shrugged. 'The old man told me that powerful magic is always hard to keep up.'

'Old man?'

'Why Fagin of course,' Dodge sighed, pulling his hat down further on his head as they strode on. 'I guess you don't know who he is either.' The boy tutted. 'Everyone in London knows who Fagin is. He's a great collector of things.'

'Well, I'm not from London, am I?' Oliver sucked back a pained gasp as he felt a loose stone, hidden in the grass, stab into his foot. 'In fact, I've been walking for seven days just so that I can get there.'

'Got family in London, have ya, Olly?'

Oliver lifted his chin proudly. 'No, not really, but I can make my own wa –'

'Nah,' Dodge interrupted. 'I didn't think you had family. Someone with family wouldn't be sleeping in a field at night, would they?'

'You were out there too,' Oliver pointed out. 'Guess you haven't got a family either.'

'I had business.' Dodge flicked up the collar of his coat. 'Important business and you're lucky that I did or you would be a woe-begotten by now.' He gave a honk of laughter. 'What were you doin' with all that standing about and clenching your fists?'

'I was –' Oliver stopped himself. He was going to say that he was trying to summon the Rage, but something stopped him. 'I was just thinking about my next move.'

'People think far too much in my opinion,' Dodge replied with all the wisdom of a sage. 'It gets you in all kind of trouble and leaves no time for action. Come on.'

Dodge continued to lead the way through the graveyard, his eyes raking over the tombstones, his face twisted in concentration. 'Aha!' he exclaimed. The boy stopped by a small, unassuming headstone and clapped his hands before rubbing them together eagerly. 'This will do, Yes, this will do nicely!'

Oliver peered at the tombstone, wishing he could read it. 'What does it say?' he asked.

Dodge knelt by the stone. 'Martha Steward,' he read out loud. 'Mother and Wife. Died 19th December 1834.'

'She was only buried here two months ago.' Oliver's throat became tight as the word mother lingered in his mind.

'I know, perfect, isn't it?' Dodge said. 'Let's dig.'

'Dig?' Oliver repeated, his voice hoarse.

'Yes, dig.' Dodge nodded. 'I was a grave-robber before Fagin found me. A foul job, I won't lie, but it taught me some useful things.' He winked. 'The earth will still be soft here. Plus, there'll still be flesh on the old girl. We'll use it to disguise our smell.'

'N-no, n-no, we can't,' Oliver stuttered. 'It's wrong.'

'Don't be troublesome, Olly. We'll dig up old Martha here, gather up her hands, mottled and grey, and wipe them on our faces. Scratch our necks and backs until they are sore.' Dodge's face lost its smile. 'We'll take her hair and plait it to our scalp, we'll loosen her teeth and put them in our pockets, and they'll rattle when we run. We'll do what we need to do to survive, and you'll help or the woe-begottens will never give up their pursuit.' The dodger's eyes flashed. 'Now dig.'

Oliver dropped to his knees, his stomach a knot of dread. He began to scrape at the grave. The dirt was wet and mushy beneath his fingertips as he thrust his hands deep, the soil pushing up beneath his fingernails so that they became dark crescent moons. Deeper and deeper they dug, until Oliver and Dodge had to lean right over the edge of the grave to continue to shovel the soil out of the pit.

Sweat trickled between Oliver's shoulder blades and the damp smell of earth filled his nostrils. Worms crawled across his palms, their bodies pink and ridged in the moonlight as they sought to make new burrows to hide in.

And then his hands touched wood.

'Aha! We've struck the treasure, mate.' Dodge knocked on the lid of the coffin with a loud rap. 'Good thing too. Those woe-begottens will be here any moment.'

Dodge jumped into the open grave and grasped the lid of the coffin. His legs bent and his back arched, but the lid would not give.

'Stop gawping and get down here, Olly.'

Oliver's feet felt rooted to the edge of the grave, but he forced himself to climb down into the pit and slid between the wall of the grave and the coffin. Bending over, his fingers found the edge of the lid.

'All right, mate, on the count of three we pull,' Dodge shouted. 'One, two, three!'

Oliver pulled, and with a protesting scream, the wooden lid began to give. He tugged again, gritting his teeth as the wood cut into his hand. With a crack, the lid flew back. Oliver ducked, but the dodger was not quick enough. The lid slammed into him, throwing him against the wall of the grave.

Dodge groaned, but Oliver made no move to help him. A fetid gust of air escaped from the coffin and surrounded him, but Oliver did not choke on it. He could not take his eyes off the woman who lay inside. Her hands were crossed demurely in her lap, and her collar looked stiff with starch. Her hair was covered by a frilly cap, but Oliver could see her face fully. It was yellow and waxy, her cheeks sunken caverns and her eyelids two bruised-looking smudges. But her lips were pulled into a gentle smile and Oliver could sense her peace as surely as he could smell her rotting body. The peace filled him with a warm light, it hugged his skin and seeped deep inside. This lady had been sad to pass, but pleased to be free from the pain that ate away at her in life. Now her bones had been taken by the earth she was happy to lie undisturbed.

Dodge gave another groan of pain. 'Olly, give me a hand, will ya?' he asked. 'I think I've broken a rib.'

Oliver turned to Dodge and helped to ease the lid off him. He held out his hand. 'Come, I'll pull you up out of the grave.'

The dodger considered his words. 'You're right. Probably best to take a piece of her and get the stench on us while we're on the move.' He leant forward into the coffin, one hand cradling his side.

Oliver shook his head and placed a hand on the dodger's chest. 'You will not disturb her.'

Dodge's eyebrows drew together in consternation. 'What you on about!' he exclaimed. 'In case you've forgotten, we've got a pack of woe-begottens on our tail. Now stop messin' about and help me pull off an arm.'

'I will not,' Oliver said, his voice rising. He could feel

the crackle of the Rage stirring. 'She is at peace and we will not disturb her.'

Dodge opened his mouth to protest, but stopped as he looked into Oliver's eyes. 'You look funny,' he said. 'Your eyes are all fierce, like. Silvery even.' Dodge let out a low whistle. 'Well, I never. Olly mate, you've been holding out on me.'

'What are you talking about?' Oliver asked.

'You're one of them.'

'Who's them?'

'A warlock. A real, bona fide, one in a million warlock.' Dodge shook his head, as if he could not quite believe it. 'I'd always figured a warlock would look more impressive, like. You know, full of unbridled power, and a fearsome wielder of fury and magic.'

'I'm just a boy.' Oliver found himself saying for the second time that week. But even as he spoke the words, he could feel the tingle of heat at his fingertips. And as the word warlock repeated in his mind, his whole body vibrated as if chiming with a forgotten song.

Dodge sighed and clutched his side more tightly. 'Be you boy or warlock, Oliver, if you will not let us smother ourselves in the stench of decay, then you must deal with the woe-begottens. We can't carry on running and I won't be able to turn us to smoke for a while. I'm all out of puff.'

Oliver swallowed hard. 'I will deal with them,' he said.

A moan pierced the air, soon joined by another and then another until there was a chorus of wailing and it was getting closer.

Dodge stared hard at him. 'Time to show what you're made of.'

Chapter IX

Where Oliver faces the woe-begottens

Oliver scrambled out of the grave. Dodge pulled himself up as well so that he was standing beside him. In the distance, Oliver could see the jerky, stilted movements of the woe-begottens staggering towards him. Their bodies, though strangely knotted and contorted did not break pace once.

Dodge was right – they would never cease in their pursuit. Oliver held his hands out, waiting for a bolt of energy to burst forth from his fingertips. But nothing came. He could feel the Rage simmering within, but no sparks lit his fingertips.

The woe-begottens were just a few feet away now. Their yellow, bloodshot eyes, filmy and thick with seeping mucus, fixed on Dodge and Oliver. The closest was a tall, powerfully built man with hands like hams.

Half of his face had been stripped away or eaten, and showed gum, teeth and the white arc of an eye socket, but the other half still wore a thick black beard.

It was tangled and rat-tailed now, but Oliver could sense that it had once been neatly shaped and lustrous. He knew with sudden certainty that this man had cared deeply about what his beard had looked like before . . . *Before he was bitten on his way home from the inn*, Oliver thought. *Before he could reach his cottage where his wife and children rested*.

Fragmented images sliced into Oliver's head and brought a piercing pain that exploded behind his eyes. He could see a child being dandled on a knee by a woman with a face soft with love. He could see a thatched cottage with a red door which would not be opened however much it was banged on. However much the woe-begotten with the beard had moaned and screamed at it.

He could feel the woe-begotten's despair. It lay deep beneath the hunger and the instinct to hunt. He could feel his yearning to sit by the fire and hear his wife's prattle, to see her brushing their child's hair just one more time. Deeper still, there was the desire to sleep, to stop the roaming across the countryside, the feasting on flesh, and not to be this *thing* any longer.

More thoughts slashed at Oliver from the other woe-begottens. Stories of a life before: from the young girl in the tattered dress who reached out with fingerless hands, remembering how she once used to pluck flowers from the meadow for her grandmother; memories from the old man whose back was hunched from years of working in a quarry. They pushed at Oliver like a wave, slamming into him, pressing him backwards.

'Olly, do something!' Dodge said. 'Don't just stand there.'

Oliver stared at the staggering figures that approached, at their ragged mouths, bloody and open, at their fingers clamped into claws, the sores that oozed on their faces. But he also saw the pretty lace on the ragged dress, the rosy curve of a young girl's cheek, the silvery sweep of hair on the old man's crown. Men, women and children trapped by the woe-begotten's curse. *They can't stop their hunger for flesh; they can't find peace.*

'What are you waiting for?' Dodge cried. 'You said you would deal with them, so deal with them. I'm not hanging around. I don't care what Fa –'

The boy was cut short as a woe-begotten struck out at him with a gnarled hand caked in blood and foul dirt. Instantly, Dodge's body began to flicker into smoke. 'I'm sorry, Olly,' he said. 'I'm out of here.'

The woe-begottens were right on top of them now and Oliver could see his own frightened face reflected in the yellow of their eyeballs. He took a hesitant step forward, the Rage had quietened, but not faded entirely. For the first time it whispered to him: *Give them peace, set them free*.

Oliver felt rather than ordered his hands to rise higher. His fingers traced a symbol in the air, two spirals linked by a thread. 'Rest,' he commanded. 'Peace.'

As one, the woe-begottens dropped to their knees like puppets whose strings had been cut. Their wasted knees, blue with cold and green with decay, sank into the earth and planted there. Then they began to sigh. Sighs as deep as wells, sighs so loud their bodies shook with it. Sighs of release that swirled among the gravestones, across the grass and wrapped round Oliver. He could feel their release, even as they lay down on the grass and closed their eyes, which were no longer red and yellow, but clear. The veins under their skin ceased pulsing and their tired, wrecked bodies stopped heaving. Then they were quite still.

Oliver stared at their inert bodies. He dropped his hand, confusion and relief causing his whole body to shake.

'Mate, that was some impressive workmanship.' Dodge reappeared at his side.

'I thought you'd gone off in a puff of smoke,' Oliver replied.

'You can't blame me for that.' Dodge slapped a hand on Oliver's shoulder. 'You did take your sweet old time.'

He sniffed. 'Though to kill a pack of woe-begottens by casting a symbol on the air is advanced stuff. So I forgive you.'

'I didn't kill them,' Oliver shot back. He felt sick at the idea of taking another's life. He looked at the bodies that lay on the ground. 'I set them free. It's what they wanted.'

Dodge shrugged. 'Whatever you say, but we are free of them. I owe you one, Olly.'

Dodge reached up and untied one of the pewter keys that hung round his neck. 'Fagin gave me these keys when he took me in.' Dodge held the prized possession out to Oliver. 'I've never had any other gifts, but I'd like you to have this.' Dodge looked self-conscious. 'As a thank you for saving me.'

'I don't know what to say.' Oliver looked down at the key. It was a stubby, ugly thing with strange etchings carved into its body. He found his lip curling in distaste, but quickly forced a smile on to his face. 'Dodge, that's really kind of you but . . .' he trailed off as he saw the other boy's dark eyes fill with wounded pride.

'It's all right, mate. I guess it's not much to look at, is it?' Dodge's long, thin, brown fingers closed over the key. 'I was silly to offer. I just thought you might like it because I have one as well.' His throat worked furiously.

'No,' Oliver said. 'I would love to have the key.'

A smile split Dodge's face. 'That's excellent, mate, really excellent.' He folded the key into Oliver's hand and watched expectantly.

'Right, yes, I suppose I should wear it.' Oliver lifted the key on its tattered piece of string and went to fasten it at the back of his neck. He gasped as the key touched the skin at the base of his throat. He had expected it to be cold, but not this piercing iciness that seemed to penetrate right into the marrow of his bones. The metal hung there awkwardly, feeling slimy and grasping.

Dodge was watching him closely. 'Like it?'

Oliver managed to nod once. He hugged his arms and tried to warm himself, but nothing would beat back the chill. He desperately wanted to remove the key, but didn't want to risk hurting Dodge's feelings.

'And look, you are freezing. You don't have a coat or even a shoe on your foot.' Dodge tutted sympathetically. 'Come with me. Fagin will see you right.'

'I-I-' Oliver's teeth were chattering so hard he couldn't finish his sentence.

'Come on, let's walk and you'll warm up,' Dodge encouraged. 'Back at mine, there will be a nice soft bed waiting for you and all the food you can eat. Fagin's good like that.'

Oliver had planned to say that he would not be following Dodge to Fagin's house, he wanted to make his own way in London, but the lure of food and a soft bed persuaded his feet otherwise.

No harm in sleeping in a bed for just one night, he thought to himself. *To eat something other than grass for one day. Searching for my destiny can start tomorrow.*

Oliver suddenly remembered the woe-begottens and whipped round. 'Shouldn't we bury them?' he said, angry at himself for almost forgetting them.

'Olly, you may not have noticed, but we are in a graveyard and dead people get buried in graveyards. They will be looked after. Come on. You can trust me.'

Dodge strode forward, his long coat flapping in the wind like an angry raven.

Oliver took one last look at the woe-begottens. Those corpses had been innocents before they were transformed into monsters by a bite. Their torment was ended now and Oliver felt a brief stab of envy. The woe-begottens had been released, but why did Oliver feel so trapped?

Dawn was still far from breaking when they reached the turnpike at Islington. They crossed from the Angel into St John's Road; struck down the small street which terminated at Sadler's Wells Theatre, through Exmouth Street and Coppice Row, down the little court by the side of the workhouse, across the bear-bating ground that once bore the name of Hockley-in-the-Hole and thence into Little Saffron Hill.

Dodge scudded at a rapid pace, directing Oliver to follow close at his heels. Although Oliver had enough to occupy his attention in trying to keep Dodge in sight, he could not help bestowing a few hasty glances on either side of the way as he passed along. A dirtier or more wretched place he had never seen. The street was very narrow and muddy, and the air was impregnated with filthy odours.

There were a good many small shops, but the only stock-in-trade appeared to be heaps of children who, even at that time of night, were crawling in and out of the doors, or screaming from the inside. The sole establishments that seemed to prosper amid the general blight of the place were the public-houses, and in them, man and demon drank until their eyes crossed and they sat on the side of the road singing raucous songs.

Oliver couldn't help staring at the demons as he and Dodge walked past. One creature, whose mouth was a beak and whose nose was simply a slit that seeped with pus, stared right back at him and hissed to reveal a snake's tongue studded with spikes.

Dodge yanked on Oliver's sleeve and dragged him away. 'Don't be foolish now – you can't be staring like that.'

'What was that thing?' Oliver asked.

'That was an Azhhul.' Dodge checked over his shoulder to make sure they weren't being followed. 'They are a lower class of demon, but will flay the skin off your back with a flick of their tongue before you can even blink.'

'But why are they here? Sitting in the street, drinking?' Oliver shook his head. 'Surely demons have better things to do?'

Dodge shrugged. 'I know, it's stupid. It's not like demons can even get drunk, but they are trying to be like humans, mimicking their experiences.' He shook his head. 'The thing is, the feeling is never enough. Trust me, before the end of the night that Azhhul will take possession of that poor idiot's body. He'll use it, fight with it, tear it apart if he wants.'

'Then we have to help that man,' Oliver said. 'Warn him.' He turned round.

'Olly, there's no point. That man knows what he's doing just as well as that demon, but he's choosing to take the risk to get free ale.'

'But . . .' Oliver protested.

'But nothing, come on.' Dodge walked on and Oliver followed him, guilt squirming in his stomach.

Covered ways and yards disclosed little knots of houses, where drunken men and women were positively wallowing in filth; and from several of the houses, vampyres with frayed cuffs and shoes worn down at heel cautiously emerged. Blood, salty and sweet, still glistened on their lips as they scurried home before the sun rose fully. Ill-looking men, women and children stood in their doorways and watched the vampyres leave, handkerchiefs stiff with blood clutched to their necks, coins from their bloodsucking clients jingling in their pockets.

Oliver had thought that London would be a place of wonders and opportunity. His disappointment at this sight alone was enough to make him want to turn away right now and escape this town of horrors. *But where would I go?* he asked himself.

As they reached the bottom of the hill, Dodge caught him by the arm, pushed open the door of a house near Field Lane and drew him into the passage. Closing the door behind him, Dodge whistled and then cocked his head and waited.

'Who goes there!' cried a voice from below.

'Ankou's thief,' was Dodge's reply.

This seemed to be some watchword or signal that all was right, for the light of a feeble candle gleamed on the wall at the remote end of the passage and a boy's face peeped out from where a balustrade of the old kitchen staircase had been broken away.

'There's two of you,' said the boy, thrusting the candle

further out and shielding his eyes with his hand. 'Who's t'other one, Dodge?'

'A new pal,' replied the dodger, pulling Oliver forward.

'Where did he come from?'

'Greenland. Is Fagin upstairs?'

'Yes, he's a-sortin' the wipes. Up with you!' The candle was drawn back and the face disappeared.

Oliver, groping his way with one hand and having the other firmly grasped by his companion, ascended with much difficulty the dark and broken stairs, which his conductor mounted with an ease and expedition that showed he was well acquainted with them. At the top, he threw open the door of a back room and drew Oliver in after him.

The walls and ceiling of the room were perfectly black with age and dirt, and stars and symbols were drawn in white chalk on their surface. There was a copper tub before the fire, and near that a crooked table upon which were a candle, two or three pewter pots, a loaf and butter, and a plate.

In a frying pan, which was secured to the mantelshelf over the fire by a string, some sausages were cooking. And standing over them, with a toasting fork in his hand, was a very old, shrivelled man, whose face was obscured by a quantity of matted red hair and a wide hat. He was dressed in a greasy flannel gown, and seemed to be dividing his attention between the frying pan and the clothes horse, over which a great number of silk handkerchiefs, dyed a strange maroon colour, were hanging. Piles of white handkerchiefs were stacked here and there around the room.

A rough bed made of old sacks stood at the side of the chamber and seated round the table were four or five boys, none older than the dodger, smoking long clay pipes and drinking spirits with the air of middle-aged men.

They all crowded about Dodge as he approached the old man and whispered in his ear. He then turned round and grinned at Oliver. So did the old man himself, toasting fork in hand.

'This is him, Fagin,' said Dodge. 'My friend Oliver Twisted.'

Fagin made a low bow to Oliver and took him by the hand and said he was pleased to make his acquaintance. Upon this, the young gentlemen with the pipes surrounded Oliver and took some time to examine him.

'I don't think he looks so special,' one complained. 'I don't see why we had to stay up and wait for him.'

Oliver frowned. 'How could you wait up for me?' he asked. 'You didn't know I was coming.'

'Don't mind Charley,' Fagin said swiftly. 'He doesn't know what he's saying most of the time.' The old man whacked Charley across the back of the head then shooed him and the other boys away from his guest.

'We are very glad to see you, Oliver, very,' said Fagin. 'Dodge, take off the sausages and draw the tub away from the fire so that Oliver can warm up.'

Dodge scooted forward and pulled the large copper tub into the corner. As it was dragged past him, Oliver saw that the tub was filled with a foul-looking brown, gloopy liquid and a clutch of linen squares floated on the surface.

'Ah, you're a-staring at the pocket handkerchiefs! Eh, my dear. There are a good many of 'em, ain't there? I collect them, you see.' Fagin pointed to a row of handkerchiefs that hung drying from a line in front of the fire. 'I am a collector of little things, things that weigh not a grain, and then I use them in the best way I see fit. Ain't that right, boys?'

The latter part of this speech was hailed by a boisterous shout from all the boys, after which they went through to their beds in the next room.

Oliver and Dodge ate their sausages and drank deeply from tumblers filled with water. Oliver's starving stomach protested as the food and drink hit the empty space, but he managed to hold on to the meal.

Fagin leant forward and touched the key at Oliver's neck. 'I see Dodge has given you a little gift.' In the firelight, Oliver could see Fagin's face properly for the first time as it peered out from under the brim of his hat. His eyes were set deep in their sockets and his face was gaunt and sallow. The old man's fingers touched the string and he rubbed it between his finger and thumb. 'The string is strong and won't be broken,' he murmured. 'It can't be cut or torn asunder. You understand that, don't you, Oliver? If Dodge has given you a gift, it would be wrong to take it off. You will never take it off.'

Oliver nodded even though the action didn't really feel like his own. 'I won't take it off.'

Fagin leant back and smiled, disclosing among his toothless gums a few such fangs as should have been a dog's or a rat's. It was almost as if his teeth had been filed down to fine points and Oliver felt his stomach lurch again. *I need to get away from here*, he thought.

He stood up. 'Thank you for your kindness, but I really should go.'

'Oliver, don't be ridiculous. Where would you go?' Fagin said. 'You cannot leave.'

The key became cold on Oliver's chest and it was as if a spear of ice had pierced him. He shivered despite the fire.

'You're cold,' Fagin said. 'You must get some rest. There is a nice soft bed waiting for you.'

All thoughts of leaving were chased from Oliver's head at Fagin's words. His body felt as heavy as lead and his limbs ached with tiredness.

'You'll rest with us a bit here, won't you, Olly?' Dodge said.

Oliver did not have the energy to speak and instead he felt himself guided on to the bed made of sacks, and then he sank into a deep sleep.

Chapter X

In which Oliver learns the true nature of Fagin

It was late next morning when Oliver began to awaken from the deepest of slumbers. There was no other person in the room but Fagin, who was boiling some more of the foul-smelling liquid that had been swimming in the copper tub yesterday. He was mixing it in a saucepan and whistling softly to himself as he stirred it round and round with an iron spoon.

He would stop every now and then to listen when there was the least noise below, and when he had satisfied himself, he would go on whistling and stirring again, as before.

Although Oliver had roused himself from sleep, he was not yet thoroughly awake. There is a drowsy state, between sleeping and waking, when a person dreams more in five minutes with their eyes half open, and are half conscious of everything that is passing around them. At such time, a mortal knows just enough of what his mind is doing to form some glimmering conception of his situation, and Oliver knew in that instant he was in grave danger, but knew not yet why.

Through half-closed eyes, Oliver could see Fagin over by the fire. He heard the old man's low whistling and recognised the sound of the spoon grating against the saucepan's sides. There was the creaking sound of a drawer being opened and Fagin pulled a rusty old bread knife into sight.

He then yanked up a tatty old sleeve to reveal a skeletal-looking arm. The skin appeared wasted and wrinkly, and it was crossed with shiny scars and ragged wounds that looked far newer.

Fagin eagerly put the blade to his arm and dragged it across in one firm movement. With a faint *phhhh* of tearing, the skin parted and blood bloomed. Fagin held his arm over the bubbling saucepan and, with a grunt, squeezed it hard so that a trickle of the red juice flowed into the frothing liquid. The old man watched as his blood drip-dropped into the foul broth, his head cocked to one side, mesmerised by the crimson teardrops.

With a bloody track still winding its way down Fagin's arm, he tore a strip of dirty material off a nearby cloth, bound his wound and let his sleeve fall forward once more.

Oliver was wide awake now, but instinct told him to stay quite still so that Fagin would not guess he was no longer asleep. The old man gave the saucepan another quick stir and then took it from the hearth and over to the copper tub where he poured the contents inside. He swiftly added a pile of clean, white handkerchiefs to the liquid before going over to the clothes horse and considering the row of dyed, maroon-coloured wipes that hung there.

'A H,' he said out loud, tracing the embroidered initials on the handkerchief lovingly with one filthy fingernail. 'Abigail Hopkin. No, it is not you I need today.'

His hand trailed to another handkerchief that was initialled with the letters R S. 'Robert Seymour. No, I will not bother with you yet.'

Fagin tapped his sharpened teeth and reached for another handkerchief. 'H W. Harland Whipple. Yes, it is your turn today I think, my dear parson.' Fagin swiftly unpegged the hanky and looked over at the grandfather clock in the corner of the room. 'Yes, time to come out and play.'

He then drew forth from a trapdoor in the floor a large box, which he placed carefully on the table. As Fagin lifted the lid, a sickly yellow light pooled out of the box and he reached in and gently lifted something from the interior. It was a fragment of amber set in a stone tablet. Symbols, miniature versions of those that were chalked on the ceiling, were etched into the stone.

Fagin murmured something under his breath and the air began to hum. The chalked symbols above began to pulse and showered him with white powder, while the stone tablet vibrated on the table. The yellow glow of the amber became a pillar of light that shot up to the ceiling and widened out to a flat sheet.

'Aha!' Fagin shrugged up his shoulders, and his face became distorted with a hideous grin. ''Tis time, clever Tablet of Horus, to show me the parson. Show me what he is doing right now. Never can the parson hide from old Fagin. Never will I loosen the knot, or allow him to drop for a minute. No, no, no! He is mine!'

Fagin held the filthy handkerchief in his curled fist and thrust it into the light. An image of an old man appeared in the amber screen, and with a satisfied nod, Fagin took the handkerchief away.

The old man wore a white wig, a long robe and a pair of small glasses that were perched on the end of his nose. He was standing behind a pulpit, his eyes full of fire and brimstone, and Oliver could hear the parson's voice booming at him from across the room.

''Tis true, my friends, that hell has come to earth,'

the parson cried. 'But we will stand resolute; we will not be turned from all that is good and bright in this world.' The parson stared out at his congregation. 'One day we will be delivered. The darkness will be beat back and all of its kin sent to hell where they belong. Those darkseers that sit at heads of power and take the rights of men, they will be sent back. The vampyres, the ghosts, the goblins, the piskies, the demons, the witches, the warlocks, the lupine, the ghouls. They will be sent back and we will rejoice.'

Fagin stared at the parson with a sneering expression. 'But what of the soul-stealers, my good parson? What about the puppet master who can make you dance to his very own tune?' Fagin flicked his finger and the old parson pulled off his wig and threw it to the floor to reveal a bald pate ringed by fine, wispy hair. Fagin flicked his finger again and the parson found himself on tiptoes doing a little twirl.

'I am possessed!' the parson screamed as, with another flick of his finger, Fagin had him take off his own glasses and crush them underfoot.

Fagin howled with laughter. 'Possessed indeed. I am not a base demon. I am Ankou the eater of souls, and I have yours now and no one can stop me.' He held up the handkerchief and dangled it beneath the parson's nose as if he could see it. 'This was once yours, but it was stolen from your pocket by my boys and given to me. The threads have drunk my blood, and my essence is now soaked deep into the fibres and bound to them by dark enchantment. You will never be free and when I tire of you, I will suck your soul dry and leave you a husk.'

Fagin licked his lips as if he could almost taste the preacher's soul. 'Listen now. Tonight you will take the golden cup that lies hidden in the vestibule and you will leave it outside your church to be collected. Understood?'

The preacher nodded.

'Excellent,' Fagin said. 'Off you go. You have a sermon to finish.'

The parson shuffled back to the pulpit, his face a pale sheet and his eyes dilated. He tried to address his congregation again, but the words did not come. Instead he clung to the pulpit, sobs wracking his body.

Fagin chuckled to himself as the image of the parson faded and became a clear expanse of yellow light once more. The old man wiped the tears of laughter from the corner of his eyes before reaching down and touching one of the symbols on the stone tablet and whispering a new incantation under his breath.

Instantly, a new shape started to form in the amber light. It was a giant stone wolf and in front of it stood Lord Skinim, the high priest of the Brotherhood of Fenris.

'It is about time,' the high priest said. 'You have news for me, Fagin, I hope.'

'The boy has been found and lies at this very moment asleep in my house. One of my boys, Dodge, found him yesterday exactly where you said he would be. 'Tis really quite extraordinary.'

'I am the high priest of the Brotherhood. Did you doubt my ability to locate him?'

'No, of course not, my lord. I merely meant to comment that your abilities are truly awe-inspiring.' Fagin gave a little bow and looked up grovellingly at Lord Skinim.

'I see. Well, I am pleased with your work, Fagin, and you will be paid handsomely when you hand Oliver over. However, I have decided that you would be a good tutor for young Twisted. His mind is very pure, innocent even. Keep him with you and turn his mind to evil.' Lord Skinim's eyes narrowed. 'But make sure he does not get away. You would not like to see what I did to the last guardians of Oliver who failed me.'

'Oh, Oliver will not be going anywhere.' Fagin sounded smug. 'He has been given a keeper's key by my boy, Dodge. I am now Oliver's master. Whatever I say to him he must do. Twisted will not even be able to use any power he may have unless I give my direct permission.'

'I am well aware of what a keeper's key is,' the high

priest snapped. 'But what will stop him from removing it?'

Fagin smirked. 'I have enchanted the string that ties it – I do that to all my boys. He'll never be free of it – unless I tell him to remove it.'

The high priest nodded. 'Impressive conjuring. That is not an easy enchantment. Keep the boy safe; he is essential to the downfall of the Knights of Nostradamus once and for all. Speaking of which, how does your other project go?'

Fagin looked up slyly at the high priest. 'I feel Brownlow's soul will soon be under our control.'

'Good.' The high priest bared his teeth. 'I tire of his meddling ways. He and the rest of the Knights are a constant thorn in my side and it needs to be removed.'

'As you wish, my lord,' Fagin said. 'The Knights have hunted my kind for many years. It is most satisfying to now be the hunter.'

Lord Skinim nodded. 'You succeed in getting Brownlow's soul and I will give you anything, Fagin. Anything you want.'

The high priest faded from sight and the light disappeared. Fagin carefully picked up the Tablet of Horus and deposited it into its box before returning it safely beneath the floorboards.

Oliver's mind was racing with all that he had learnt. He did not understand everything Fagin had said and done, but he knew that the soul-stealer had put an enchantment on him which meant that he could be controlled by Fagin's words.

'What a fine thing it would be to destroy the Knights and have the Brotherhood of Fenris in my debt,' Fagin murmured. 'And what would I ask for? Wealth, power?' He laughed wildly. 'No, these things I can get for myself. I would want a soul of my very own. Never have I had one, always I have been an eater of others.' Fagin hugged himself and turned in a slow circle. 'It would be a soul befitting a king.' As Fagin uttered these words, his bright, dark eyes, which had been staring vacantly before him, fell on Oliver's face and he knew at once that he had been observed.

With a surprisingly quick movement, he snatched the rusty bread knife from the table and started furiously up. 'What's that?' said Fagin. 'What do you watch me for? Why are you awake? Speak out, boy! I order you to tell me!'

'I wasn't able to sleep any longer, sir,' replied Oliver in as meek a voice as he could. 'I am very sorry if I have disturbed you, sir.'

'You were not awake an hour ago?' said Fagin, scowling fiercely at him. 'I demand you tell me the truth.'

Oliver could feel the coldness of the key on his chest, which spread, encircling his ribs. Even at the thought of lying, his chest constricted and it felt like his bones would be crushed into powder. Oliver knew he could not lie; the truth was being squeezed out of him.

'No! No, indeed!' he said. 'I was not awake an hour ago.'

'Are you sure?' cried Fagin with a still fiercer look than before and a threatening attitude.

'Upon my word I was not, sir,' replied Oliver truthfully, for he had not been awake an hour earlier. He prayed that Fagin would not ask if he had witnessed anything else because he realised that he would not be able to lie.

'Tush, tush, my dear Oliver,' said Fagin, abruptly resuming his old manner, and playing with the knife a little before he laid it down – as if to induce the belief that he had caught it up in mere sport. 'Of course I believe you. You had to tell me the truth as I asked you a direct question.'

'I will get up now, if I may,' Oliver said, scared that Fagin might question him further.

'Certainly, certainly,' replied the soul-stealer. 'There's a pitcher of water in the corner by the door. Bring it here and I'll give you a basin to wash your face in.'

Oliver got up, walked across the room and stooped for an instant to raise the pitcher. His eyes rested on the maroon-coloured handkerchiefs that hung on the clothes horse and he swallowed hard as he now understood their purpose. Fagin had control of all these poor souls and now he controlled Oliver as well.

He had scarcely washed his face and made everything tidy by emptying the basin out of the window at Fagin's insistence when the dodger returned, accompanied by Charley Bates, whom Oliver recognised as one of the smoking boys from the previous night.

The four sat down to eat some hot rolls and ham, which Dodge had brought home in the crown of his hat, but Oliver noticed that even though Fagin tore the rolls into strips and cut his ham into cubes, he did not let a morsel pass his lips.

'Well,' said Fagin, glancing shrewdly at Oliver and then addressing himself to Dodge, 'I hope you've been hard at work this morning?'

'Hard,' replied the dodger.

'As nails,' added Charley Bates.

'Good boys, good boys!' said Fagin. 'What have you got, Dodge?'

'A couple of wallets,' replied that young gentleman.

'Lined?' enquired Fagin, with eagerness. 'Initialled?'

'Indeed,' replied Dodge, producing two wallets, one green and the other red.

'Not so heavy as they might be,' said Fagin, after

looking at the insides carefully. 'But very neatly and nicely made. Ingenious workman the dodger is, ain't he, Oliver?'

Oliver had to swallow a snort. Fagin really meant him to believe that Dodge had made the wallets. He was beginning to realise just how naive, Fagin thought he must be. *So be it. I will pretend to be as stupid as they think I am until I can discover a way to get rid of this key and make my escape.*

'Very well made indeed, sir,' said Oliver. At which Charley Bates laughed uproariously. Dodge remained quiet though and studied Oliver closely.

'And what have you got, Charley?' said Fagin.

'Wipes,' replied the boy, at the same time producing four pocket handkerchiefs.

'My favourite,' said Fagin, inspecting them closely. He frowned. 'But these are not correct. Where are the initials? How are we to know if they are the true article? How am I to do my work?'

Charley's face went pale. 'I hit the mark as you said, Fagin. It ain't my fault they weren't initialled.'

Fagin's nostrils flared. 'I do not like the way you respond, Charley. Your tone irks me.'

'Sorry, sir.' Charley's head was bowed. 'Please don't punish me.' His trembling fingers went to the key at his neck.

'Tush, tush, punish, as if I would,' Fagin said quickly. ''Tis well. We will have to start again with these wipes and get new ones that are appropriate.' The old man clapped his hands. 'Perhaps we'll teach Oliver how to do it. Shall we, Oliver, eh? Ha ha ha!'

'If you please, sir,' said Oliver in his most eager voice.

'You'd like to be able to make pocket handkerchiefs appear as easy as Charley Bates, wouldn't you,' Fagin said.

'Very much indeed, if you'll teach me, sir,' replied Oliver.

Charley Bates burst into another laugh, forcing the water he was drinking to go down the wrong channel, very nearly resulting in his premature suffocation.

'He is so jolly green!' said Charley when he recovered, by way of an apology to the company for his impolite behaviour.

Dodge said nothing, but he looked at Oliver with a wry smile on his lips. 'Olly, I wonder if you're as green as you're making out,' he said softly. 'We'll know better, by and by.'

Oliver held Dodge's eyes and smiled back. He refused to let his hurt or anger at Dodge's betrayal for bringing him to this place show on his face.

'If I am to stay here as Fagin says I must, then I have to learn how to make my contribution just as you all do.' Oliver shrugged. 'That's fine with you, isn't it, Dodge?'

Fagin slapped a hand on Oliver's shoulder. 'My dear boy, of course that is fine,' he said. 'Let me share with you a game. We play it often to amuse ourselves, I wonder how well you will do with it.'

Oliver watched as Fagin, Charley and Dodge embarked on a rather strange performance.

Fagin buttoned his coat tight round him and, putting his spectacle case and handkerchief in his pockets, trotted up and down the room with a stick, in imitation of the manner in which old gentlemen walk about the streets any hour in the day. Sometimes he stopped at the fireplace, and sometimes at the door, making believe that he was staring with all his might into shop windows. At such times, he would look constantly round him, for fear of thieves, and would keep slapping all his pockets in turn, to see that he hadn't lost anything, in such a very funny and natural manner that Oliver found himself laughing despite himself.

All this time, the two boys followed him closely about, getting out of his sight so nimbly, every time he turned round, that it was impossible to follow their motions. At last, Dodge trod upon his toes, while Charley Bates stumbled up against him from behind; and in that one moment they took from him with the most extraordinary rapidity the handkerchief and spectacle case.

Oliver stopped laughing as he saw the handkerchief

in Dodge's hand. It was such a small thing, this bit of cloth, but in Fagin's hands it was a soul that would not be freed until it had delivered all that it could, and would then be consumed. Just like the poor preacher Oliver had seen earlier.

'There, my dear Oliver,' said Fagin. 'That's the game and Dodge and Charley are the best at it.' He patted the two boys on the shoulder. 'Make 'em your models.'

Oliver nodded.

'Let's see how fast a learner you are, young Oliver.' Fagin came to stand next to him. 'Is my handkerchief hanging out of my pocket?' he asked, stopping short.

'Yes, sir,' said Oliver.

'See if you can take it out without my feeling it; as you saw them do.'

Oliver had to hold his body as tight as a bowstring to stop himself shuddering as he approached Fagin. He held up the bottom of the pocket with one hand, as he had seen the dodger do, and drew the handkerchief lightly out of it with the other hand.

'Is it gone?' cried Fagin.

'Here it is, sir,' said Oliver, showing it in his hand.

'You're a clever boy,' said Fagin, patting Oliver on the head approvingly. 'I never saw a sharper lad.'

'Or a wolf in sheep's clothing,' Dodge muttered.

Fagin ignored him. 'Maybe I will let you go out with

Charley and Dodge one day. You have an innocent-looking face that could help our cause.' The old man nodded to himself.

'Come, show me again how you would take the handkerchief.'

Chapter XI

In which Oliver comes to understand the key and Fagin's power a little better

A few days passed and Oliver took the time to study Fagin and his young companions closely. Each day, he hoped that he might be able to find a means of escape from the soul-stealer and the keeper's key.

Oliver saw that each boy had a key round his neck, including the dodger, who had clearly only worn a second key so that he could give it to Oliver on the night they met. From what he could see, none of the boys could take the key off, but the further away Fagin was, the more time it took for the key to exercise its control. It seemed that Fagin did not control all the thoughts and movements of the boys, but rather once he issued a command, it could not be refused.

Or could it . . .?

Oliver was sitting at the main table and he was

forming a plan. It was not a complex plan, or even a plan that had a hell's mouth chance of working, but he had to try it. He needed to get out of the house and away from Fagin. *Really far away*, Oliver thought, *and maybe then the key won't have enough power to control me.* He glanced over at the soul-stealer who was by the fire drying handkerchiefs. The problem was the old man didn't let Oliver out of his sight ever.

There was a clatter of footsteps on the stairs and Dodge and the boys came back to Fagin's den with their heads hung low. Their pockets were quite empty, with no handkerchiefs to be seen at all.

'The mark you sent us after is too wily,' Charley Bates complained. 'Every time we close in, he slips away like he senses the danger.'

'This is no small fish I have asked you to reel in,' Fagin snapped. 'Brownlow is the head of the London chapter of the Knights of Nostradamus. His powers of self-preservation are well honed.' The old man rolled back his sleeve and scratched vigorously at the cuts that lanced his arm, his curved, dirty fingernails tearing at the scabs on his skin until the wounds ran once more in a plaited rope of blood and pus. 'Still, it is vital that we get a handkerchief or wallet from him.' Fagin's eyes scanned the room as if looking for inspiration. They eventually came to rest on Oliver. 'We need another approach, a face that will not arouse suspicion. Oliver could do nicely.' Fagin looked thoughtful. 'But do I risk one prize to gain another?'

'I would be pleased to help,' Oliver interjected. Inside, his heart was hammering hard. It was the slimmest of chances to escape, but he had to grab it. 'You have looked after me so well, it is the least I can do.'

Dodge snorted. 'Laying it on a bit thick, don't you think, Olly?' He turned to Fagin. 'This one is trying to pull the wool over our eyes. I told you what I saw him do to those woe-begottens.'

'Those powers have been contained,' Fagin muttered. 'Besides, you leave me little choice, Dodge. I need that handkerchief. I fear I might be in serious trouble without it.' The old man crossed his scrawny arms. 'If I die, Dodge, who will feed and clothe all your little friends? Who will do that if not I?' Fagin cocked his head to one side, his face quizzical.

'No one,' Dodge said.

'That's correct. Take Oliver with you when you go out now and let him help you. But treasure him – he is worth more than you know.'

'I don't see why he is such a prize,' Charley Bates said. 'He is just a boy.'

Dodge shook his head. 'No, Charley, he's more than that. He's a pain in the backside. Come on, let's go.'

'Yes, Dodge,' Oliver said, trying to keep his voice level and even.

The three boys sallied out, the dodger with his coat-sleeves tucked up and his hat cocked as usual, Charley Bates sauntering along with his hands in his pockets, and Oliver between them, wondering when he might put his plan of escape into action.

They were just emerging from a narrow court not far from the open square in Clerkenwell when the dodger made a sudden stop and, laying his finger on his lip, drew his companions back again, with the greatest caution and circumspection.

'What's the matter?' demanded Oliver.

'Hush!' replied the dodger. 'Do you see him at the bookstall?'

'The old gentleman over the way?' said Oliver. 'Yes, I see him.'

'That's Brownlow,' said the dodger. 'Just who we want.'

'He's not going to get away again,' said Charley Bates. 'Go on, Oliver, go over there and take his handkerchief.' Charley curled his lip. 'Fagin seems to think you'd be useful.'

Oliver rolled his eyes. 'I was green once, Charley, but I'm learning fast. I'm not skilled enough to take the wipe without him noticing, but I could distract him if you like?'

Charley nodded. 'I like how you're thinking, Twisted.'

Oliver stepped forward, but Dodge caught his arm. 'Don't think to double-cross us, mate. It will be worse for you and the rest of us if you do. Fagin is not kind when thwarted and he knows some dangerous people.'

Oliver shrugged. 'Fine, you go and distract Brownlow then.'

Dodge shook his head. 'He knows my face well enough now I warrant. You go, but heed my warning and do not think to run. Fagin will get you back – he has his ways – you can't escape him. Trust me.'

Oliver remembered the last time Dodge had asked for his trust, just before he brought him into Fagin's clutches. He threw off Dodge's arm and half wished the Rage to come upon him, but then remembered that the key round his neck would not allow it.

Oliver straightened his shoulders. He was without his magic but not guile. Dodge said there was no escape from Fagin, but he had to try. Oliver stepped towards the old gentleman, not yet clear what his next move was, but knowing that the time had come to put his plan into action.

The man had a very respectable-looking personage, with a powdered head and gold spectacles. He was dressed in a bottle-green coat with a black velvet collar, wore white trousers and carried a smart bamboo cane under his arm, the tip of which was crowned with a silver unicorn and a dragon. Brownlow had taken up a book from the stall and there he stood, reading away, as hard as if he were in his elbow chair in his own study.

'Excuse me, sir,' Oliver said. 'I wonder if I can ask you something?'

The old man peered at Oliver over the rim of his gold spectacles. 'You are free to ask, young man,' he replied. 'But I cannot promise that I will be able to answer your question.'

'Are you Mr Brownlow, sir?' Oliver asked.

Brownlow frowned. 'Why, yes I am. How do you know my name?'

Over Brownlow's shoulder, Oliver could see that Dodge was just a few paces away, ready to plunge his hand into the gentleman's pocket and draw from thence a handkerchief.

'Do you know what a soul-stealer is?' Oliver asked urgently.

Mr Brownlow's bushy white eyebrows shot upwards. 'I do indeed. They are rare creatures, almost extinct I thought, stamped out!'

Dodge was just two steps away now, his face a study of concentration.

'Well, there is one in London, sir, and he is after your soul, so take care and always look over your shoulder.'

And with that, Oliver leapt to his left and threw himself into the hotchpotch of streets.

In the very instant when Oliver began to run, Brownlow spun round to see Dodge's hand in his pocket. Dodge released the wipe and instantly made ready to bolt, but Brownlow was quicker and caught him by the collar.

'Let me go!' Dodge yelled. He began to blink rapidly and then his body shifted into smoke and rose upwards, scudding away at a rapid pace in the same direction as Oliver. Charley Bates watched all this from a quiet corner and easily slunk away and lost himself in the darkness of one of the door frames.

'Stop thief!' Brownlow roared. He pointed in the direction that Dodge had fled. 'Stop the boy! Stop the thief!' There was magic in the words that Brownlow spoke and it touched all those that were in earshot. The tradesman left his counter and the car man his waggon; the butcher threw down his tray and the baker his basket; the milkman put aside his pail, the errand boy his parcels and the schoolboy his marbles. Away they ran, pell-mell, helter-skelter, slap-dash: tearing, yelling, screaming, knocking down the bystanders as they turned the corners, rousing up the dogs and astonishing the fowls. And streets, squares and courts re-echoed with the sound of the mob hunting for a boy who was fleeing. Hunting for Oliver, as Dodge remained a cloud of smoke.

'Stop thief! Stop thief!' The cry was taken up by a hundred voices, and the crowd accumulated at every turning. Away they flew, splashing through the mud and rattling along the pavements: up went the windows, out ran the people, onward bore the mob. An entire public house deserted their plates and tankards and joined the rushing throng, swelling the shout and lending fresh vigour to the cry, 'Stop thief! Stop thief!'

Oliver could feel them behind him. He could feel their hunger to catch him. Large drops of perspiration streamed down his face. He strained every muscle to pull away from his pursuers; but they followed on his heels and gained upon him every instant, hailing his decreasing strength with joy.

Oliver felt something strike him across the side of his head and he was down upon the pavement, his skull crashing on the ground. The crowd eagerly gathered round him, each newcomer jostling and struggling with his neighbour to catch a glimpse.

'Stand aside!'

'Give him a little air!'

'Nonsense! He don't deserve it.'

'Where's the gentleman?'

'Here he is, coming down the street.'

'Make room there for the gentleman!'

'Is this the boy, sir? The boy who tried to thieve from you?'

The old gentleman was brought into the circle by the foremost of the pursuers and saw Oliver lying there, covered with mud and dust, and bleeding from a wound on his temple.

'No, this is not he,' said Brownlow, outraged. 'This is the boy who warned me.'

'He was probably in on it,' one in the crowd said. 'These thieves work in gangs.'

Brownlow stared down at Oliver. 'I do not think this is the case.' His brow creased. 'He is hurt.'

'*I* did that, sir,' said a great lubberly fellow, stepping forward. 'And I cut my knuckle striking him at his temple, yet I stopped him, sir.'

The fellow touched his hat with a grin, expecting something for his pains, but the old gentleman eyed him with an extreme expression of dislike instead.

Brownlow knelt down beside Oliver. 'Do you think you can stand?' He held out his arm. Oliver reached out his hand and gripped it and tried to get up, but a wave of nausea sent him slipping to the floor once more. His head ached and his whole body was shaking.

'Poor boy, this is all my fault!' said Brownlow, leaning over him. 'Call a coach, somebody. Directly!'

A coach was obtained and Oliver, having been carefully laid on the seat, was accompanied by Brownlow who sat opposite. The gentleman then tapped the roof of the coach with his cane. 'Driver, go! There is no time to lose.' For a moment, Oliver's eyes opened and through the window he caught a glimpse of a boy in a tall hat and a coat that was too big watching him intently as the coach rattled away.

Chapter XII

In which Oliver is taken better care of than ever he was before

The coach hurtled over nearly the same ground as that which Oliver had traversed when he first entered London in the company of the dodger and, turning a different way when it reached the Angel at Islington, stopped at length before a neat house, in a quiet, shady street near Pentonville. Here a bed was prepared, without loss of time, in which Brownlow saw his young charge carefully and comfortably deposited, and here he was tended with a kindness that Oliver had never known.

But for many days Oliver remained insensible to all the goodness of his new friends. His skull had been fractured and the blow to the temple had bruised his brain. The sun rose and sank, and rose and sank again, and many times after that, and still the boy lay stretched on his uneasy bed, dwindling away beneath the dry and wasting heat of fever.

Oliver had reached the crossroads of life and death and found himself in a field, much like the one where he had first met Dodge. There were no woe-begottens to be seen here, just a woman in a threadbare cloak and a frilly blue bonnet. She waved at him and Oliver found himself waving back.

The woman walked slowly towards him, gingerly, as if she had not walked for some time. The blue bonnet obscured the woman's face, but he could see the golden curls that rested on her shoulder.

'Oliver, what are you doing here?' the woman asked when she was just a few steps away. Her voice was soft and lilting, but threaded with exasperation.

'Where *is* here?' he asked.

'This is Otherwhere,' the woman replied. 'A waiting station for souls who cannot rest.' Her voice became like the crackle of dying embers in the grate. 'Oliver, this non-place is for the dead.'

Oliver felt his eyes burn. 'Then this is what I must be. I must be dead.'

'Dead?' the woman was outraged. 'No, it is not your time yet. Your body is tired and broken, but it still fights. It is your mind that has given up.'

'It's not my mind any more, it is Fagin's. He can

control it whenever he wants,' Oliver said bitterly.

'Then you must learn how to take your thoughts back, take control of your own destiny,' said the woman.

A strong gust of wind sprang up and disturbed the ears of wheat in the field, sending up a rustling noise that sounded like the swish of a skirt. A lone whistle echoed through the air.

'Go now, Oliver. You must return before he comes.'

'He?' Oliver said.

'Go.'

'But who are you?' Oliver asked.

The woman leant forward and pushed a lock of hair from his forehead. 'You don't know, dear heart, you really don't know?'

Weak, and thin, and pallid, Oliver finally awoke from his dream. Raising himself in the bed, he looked around. 'What room is this? Where have I been brought to?' he asked. He uttered these words in a quiet voice, but they were overheard at once. The curtain at the bed's head was hastily drawn back by a motherly old lady, who was very neatly and precisely dressed.

'Hush, my dear,' said the old lady softly. 'My name is Mrs Bedwin. You are at Mr Brownlow's home. You must lie down, or you will be ill again. You have been very bad – as bad as bad could be.'

'I had a dream,' Oliver murmured as he lay his head on the pillow. 'But I can't remember it.'

'That was the fever, my dear,' said the old lady mildly. 'It gives you strange dreams, then robs you of them.'

'I suppose it was,' replied Oliver.

The old lady made no reply to this, but brought some cool beverage for Oliver to drink. She then patted him on the cheek and told him once more that he must lie very quiet, or he would be ill again.

So Oliver kept very still, his thoughts whirring with what he should do next. He was in Brownlow's house, Mrs Bedwin had confirmed that, but what would Brownlow do with him if he knew that the Brotherhood wanted to use Oliver as a weapon against the Knights of Nostradamus?

Soon after this, Oliver dozed off again. When he awoke again, it was nearly twelve o'clock. And thus the night crept slowly on. Oliver lay awake for some time, counting the little circles of light which the reflection of the rushlight shade threw upon the ceiling, or tracing with his eyes the intricate patterns on the wall. He realised after a moment that they were symbols, but not like the ones that Oliver had seen in Fagin's den, which had been all sharp angles and points.

The symbols here were all round, circles and spirals that flowed into each other as naturally as a river joining the sea. They looked newly drawn and Oliver wondered if they had been put there to help him recover. Death had been hovering in this room for many days and nights and Oliver knew he almost hadn't made it.

Gradually, he fell into that deep, tranquil sleep, which ease from recent suffering alone imparts, that calm and peaceful rest that it is painful to wake from.

The next morning Brownlow came in as brisk as need be. He raised his spectacles on his forehead and thrust his hands behind the skirts of his dressing gown to take a good long look at Oliver.

Oliver jumped up from the chair in which he was sitting and held out his hand. His legs trembled at the sudden movement, but he forced himself to stand straight. 'Sit down, boy!' said Brownlow, after shaking his hand. 'I don't want you keeling over and breaking any of my furniture.'

Oliver gratefully sat down.

'How do you feel?' Brownlow asked.

'Much better than when you found me, sir,' replied Oliver. 'Thank you very much for your goodness to me.'

'There is no need for thanks, boy, but it would be good to have your name. After all, you seemed to know mine.'

Oliver flushed at this. 'My name is Oliver, sir, Oliver Twisted.'

'Nice to meet you, young Oliver, but I'm afraid that your name isn't the only question I am going to ask you today.'

'No, sir,' Oliver replied.

'You warned me about the soul-stealer. Will you tell me who he is and why he wants me?'

'His name is Fagin, sir. He collects handkerchiefs and then uses them to control people.' Oliver swallowed hard. 'I think he wanted to control you as well.'

'And why were you with him? Are you a thief as well, Oliver? A stealer of souls?' Brownlow's eyes were chips of hard emerald. Oliver hated to think what they might look like if Brownlow ever discovered the truth about him and the Brotherhood's plan to make him a weapon to destroy the Knights of Nostradamus once and for all.

'I am not, sir,' Oliver replied, choosing his words carefully. 'I ran away from a workhouse and I was found by one of Fagin's pupils, a boy called Dodge. I have been searching for a way to leave ever since.'

Brownlow pointed at the key round Oliver's neck. 'And where did you get this key?'

'Dodge gave it to me,' Oliver explained. 'All of Fagin's boys have one.'

'Do you know what this key does?'

Oliver remembered all too well Fagin's gleeful explanation to Lord Skinim about the power of the keeper's key, but he knew he could not mention anything to do with the Brotherhood to Brownlow.

'I do not, sir,' Oliver said, his voice hoarse around the lie.

'It is a keeper's key,' Brownlow said. 'It is used to exert control over a person.' He frowned. 'We have tried to remove it, but I'm afraid the string has been charmed. Nothing will cut through it.'

'Does that mean Fagin will always be able to command me to do things? Why hasn't he summoned me back to him already?' Oliver whispered.

'He cannot control you here,' Brownlow reassured him. 'As long as you stay in my house, you will be safe from him.'

'But sir,' Oliver asked timidly, 'why would you do this? Why would you want to help me?'

Brownlow laughed. 'It is a good question, young Oliver. My associates will think me soft hearted, foolhardy even.' He stared at Oliver hard. 'But there is something about you that reminds me of someone who was once very dear to me, and I find my curiosity piqued about your abilities.' He pointed at the key. 'The symbols carved on that foul object do not just speak of control of your thoughts. They show a need to control a great magic. Is that what you have, Oliver? A great magic?'

Fear spiked through Oliver. He did not want

Brownlow to think he could be a weapon. 'I have no magic, sir. I am just a boy.'

Brownlow scratched his chin. 'We'll see about that. Maybe your abilities haven't manifested yet – they tend to emerge in the thirteenth year. But once they do, the key's power will confine your magic. Still, I see great potential in you beyond conjuring. You are a brave soul, Oliver. Rest now, your training will begin when you are fully well.'

'Training?'

'I am a Knight of Nostradamus,' Brownlow said, drawing himself up to his full height. 'And you, Oliver, will be my new apprentice.'

Chapter XIII

Here tells of what happened to Dodge and
Charley after Oliver was put in Brownlow's
carriage, and introduces Bill Sikes and Nancy

As Oliver was being driven to Brownlow's house
after the blow to his temple, Dodge and Charley
had with great speed run through a most
intricate maze of narrow streets and courts and come to
a low and dark archway. Having remained silent here,
just long enough to recover breath to speak, Charley
Bates uttered an exclamation of amusement and delight.
Bursting into an uncontrollable fit of laughter, he
flung himself upon a doorstep and rolled thereon in a
transport of mirth.

'What's the matter with you?' enquired the dodger.

'Ha ha ha!' roared Charley Bates.

'Hold your noise,' the other boy snapped, looking
cautiously round. 'Do you want to be grabbed, stupid?'

'I can't help it,' said Charley. 'I can't help it! To see all those people running after Oliver. Him splitting away at that pace, cutting round the corners and knocking up against the posts.' He again rolled upon the doorstep and laughed louder than before.

'Will you be laughing so loudly when we tell Fagin that we've lost Oliver?' enquired Dodge, taking advantage of the next interval of breathlessness on the part of his friend to pose the question.

'What?' repeated Charley Bates.

'Ah, what indeed?' said the dodger. Taking off his hat, he scratched at his tightly curled black hair.

'Why, what would he say?' asked Charley, stopping rather suddenly in his merriment for the dodger's manner was impassive. 'What would he say?'

Dodge sighed. 'He would say be scared, Charley.' He played with the key round his neck. 'If I could run away, I would.'

'But can't Fagin just use the key to order Oliver to come back?' Charley asked. 'That's what he's done whenever one of the boys has tried to run away before.'

'Somehow, I don't think it is going to be that easy,' Dodge replied. 'Brownlow is a Knight of Nostradamus. Fagin's charm might not work in his domain. Come on, let's go.' He put his hat on again, turned on his heel and slunk down the court. Charley Bates followed, dragging his feet.

*

The noise of footsteps on the creaking stairs, a few minutes after the occurrence of this conversation, roused Fagin as he sat by the fire with his meal of a sodden and bloodied handkerchief. The material had been cut into precise small squares and in the low firelight they glistened on the tin plate like cubes of raw meat.

There had been a smile of excitement and anticipation on Fagin's face as he had raised a moistened square to his lips, but now he swiftly turned round and looked sharply out from under his thick red eyebrows. He jumped up, bent his ear towards the door and listened.

'Why, how's this?' muttered Fagin, taking a step back. 'Only two of 'em? Where's the third?'

The footsteps approached nearer. They had reached the landing. The door was slowly opened and Dodge and Charley Bates entered, closing it behind them.

'Where's Oliver?' said Fagin, with a menacing look.

Charley Bates looked uneasily at Dodge, while the other boy just stared at his feet. Neither made a reply.

'What's become of the boy?' said Fagin, seizing the dodger tightly by the collar. 'Speak out or I swear I'll eat your soul.' Fagin was shaking with rage. 'I'll suck it from your body like a yolk from an egg! Don't think I won't do it.' Fagin's mouth began to open wide, much wider than any man's mouth should, and Charley could see row upon row of razor-sharp teeth right at the back of Fagin's jaw. The inside of his throat was black with decay and reeked of rot.

Charley, who deemed it prudent in all cases to be on the safe side, and who conceived it by no means improbable that it might be his turn to be devoured next, dropped upon his knees and raised a loud, well-sustained and continuous cry, something like a mad centaur that had been speared through the side.

'Will you speak?' thundered Fagin. His voice echoed in his horribly stretched mouth, which with each passing second was coming ever closer to Dodge's face.

'Brownlow's got him and that's all about it.' Dodge's face was sullen. 'Come, let go o' me, will you! You'll get no nourishment takin' my soul this way.' With a jerk, Dodge swung himself clean out of his big coat which he left in Fagin's hands. He then snatched up the plate full of bloodied squares and waved them under Fagin's nose. 'Old man, eat something, you might be less grumpy.' Dodge raised an eyebrow. 'Start thinking right. We've got to figure out how to get Oliver back.'

Fagin stepped forward with more agility than could have been anticipated in a man of his apparent decrepitude and seized the plate from Dodge. He shovelled the squares into his cavernous mouth and soon the wet gulping sound of Fagin consuming his meal filled the room.

Charley Bates's cry had become just a whimper and, as the last piece of sodden material hit Fagin's gullet, the soul-stealer's appearance changed. For a moment, he became a young woman. The girl's eyes were wide and scared, but then became milky and flat as all colour left her skin and her face went slack.

There was a loud burp and the girl disappeared. Fagin stood in front of Dodge once more, as straight as a board, his back no longer hunched, his face not as lined.

'How was dinner?' Dodge asked, doing his best to sound jovial. If he spoke loudly and brightly, maybe he could ignore the voice in his head that whispered sadly about the girl whose soul had just been consumed. Fagin must have become bored with merely controlling her and had decided to eat her soul entirely. She would now lie in an eternal slumber, alive but not awake.

As hard as he tried, Dodge could not bury his guilt. It rose like a tide in his chest and his nails bit into his palms as he fought to hide his upset.

'Pleasant enough.' Fagin licked his lips as his mouth closed to its normal size. 'But just because I've fed does not make me forget you lost the lad.' Picking up the plate, he hurled it at Dodge's head. The dodger was too quick and ducked.

'Why, what the blazes is in the wind now!' growled a deep voice. 'Who pitched that plate at me? It's well it missed or I'd have settled somebody.' The man who snarled out these words was now standing where Dodge had been moments before.

He was a stoutly-built fellow of about thirty-five, in a black coat, very soiled drab breeches, lace-up half-boots and grey cotton stockings which enclosed a bulky pair of legs, with large, swelling calves. He had a brown hat on his head and a dirty spotted handkerchief round his neck. With the long frayed ends of this, he smeared something wet from his face, revealing, when he had done so, a broad, heavy countenance with a thick beard and two piercing eyes, one of which glinted menacingly and stared with a fixed gaze.

Something very much like fear crossed Fagin's face.

'Sikes, it has been a long time. Apologies, I did not hear you enter.'

'Course you didn't, you were too busy screaming at these two, weren't you?'

As he spoke, a white shaggy wolf with his face scratched and torn in twenty different places skulked into the room.

'Where've you been, Bullseye?' said Sikes to the wolf.

The wolf yapped back a response.

'You're getting too proud to own me afore company, are you? Lie down!'

This command was accompanied by a kick, which sent the animal to the other end of the room. The wolf appeared well used to it though, for he coiled himself up in a corner very quietly and surveyed the apartment with one red, very ill-looking eye that winked about twenty times in a minute. His other eye appeared to be sewn shut. If there ever was a perfect name for such a beast, it was Bullseye.

'What's the row?' said Sikes, seating himself deliberately. 'Bawling and scaring these boys. I wonder they don't murder you! Lucky I was never your 'prentice or I'd have done it long ago.' Sikes gave a bark of laughter. 'And before you ask, no, I couldn't have sold you afterwards. Your skin dried and crushed might have some magical potency, but I doubt it. You'd be fit for nothing but keeping as a curiosity of ugliness in a glass bottle, and I suppose they don't blow glass bottles large enough.'

'You seem out of humour, Bill,' said Fagin.

'Perhaps I am,' replied Sikes. 'I'm homeless and Nancy doesn't know yet.' He scowled. 'Work has dried up. Seems like people want to do their own killing instead of using the Wolfman to solve their problems.' He crossed his arms. 'I will be living here from now on.'

Bill Sikes looked at Fagin daring him to argue.

The soul-stealer opened his mouth to object, but then thought better of it. 'Bill, you are welcome, and Nancy as well. Indeed, I could do with having you around. I need your help.'

'Tell me what the row is.'

'I had a boy in my possession,' Fagin said softly. 'The Brotherhood of Fenris has a keen interest in him – said he could be a great weapon one day.' Fagin shot a filthy look at Dodge and Bates. 'The Brotherhood left him in my care, but these two lost him.'

'I told you that he should be left behind,' Dodge snapped back. 'If you hadn't been so keen to get Brownlow's wipe, perhaps –'

There was a heavy thud as Sikes put his boots caked with mud, and something else that Fagin cared not to think of, on the table. 'The Brotherhood was going to pay a good price, I warrant,' Sikes said. His voice cracked somewhat when he said the word Brotherhood.

'Indeed they were,' Fagin replied bitterly. 'And they are not going to be pleased to discover he is gone.' The soul-stealer shook his head. 'Now Oliver is in Brownlow's domain I will not be able to command him to come back, of that I'm sure. He'll be protected.'

'Then it is a good thing that I am here,' Sikes said. 'I will help get him back for a big enough cut of the reward.'

Fagin's pale faced twitched at this but he did not say a word.

'Tell me how he was taken,' Sikes demanded.

Dodge sighed, but quickly explained the cause and manner of Oliver's capture with such alterations and improvements on the truth, as to the dodger appeared most advisable under the circumstances.

'It will be impossible to get him back,' said Fagin. 'Brownlow's home will have impressive defences.'

'That's very likely,' returned Sikes with a malicious grin. 'But I have a plan.'

'And I'm afraid, you see,' added Fagin, speaking as if he had not noticed the interruption, and regarding the other closely as he did so, 'I'm afraid that if the Brotherhood were to show their ire to me, it could come out rather badly for everyone who knows me and especially someone like you. They have no fondness for your species, descendants of Sköll, the banished son of Fenris.'

Sikes started and turned round upon Fagin. But the soul-stealer's shoulders were shrugged up to his ears and his eyes were vacantly staring at the opposite wall.

There was a long pause.

'Old man, I do not appreciate veiled threats,' Sikes growled. 'Or a history lesson. I said I have a plan.' He punched a massive fist into his hand. 'But you will give me a cut, understood?'

Fagin grimaced, but nodded. 'So what is the plan, Bill?'

'All in good time. I don't like explaining myself twice.' Sikes nodded at Charley. 'Go fetch Nancy from the inn and tell her we're living here at Fagin's. Warn her that I don't want to hear any of her complaining.'

Charley nodded and in no time at all, he was back with the young lady. 'Why are your faces all so glum?' Nancy asked as she sailed into the room, her red gown swaying and her green boots clip-clopping across the boards. 'And why has Charley dragged me from the inn and run back here like hell's hounds are on his heels?'

'Nancy, my dear,' said Fagin in a soothing manner. 'How are you?'

'No use a-trying it on, Fagin,' replied Nancy, her dark curls bobbing. 'What have the two of you got cooking?'

'What do you mean by that?' said Sikes, looking up in a surly manner.

'What I say, Bill,' replied the lady unflinchingly.

'Why, if we did have a job going, you're just the very person for it,' reasoned Sikes. 'Nobody really knows your face.'

'And as I don't want 'em to neither,' replied Nancy in the same composed manner. 'It's rather more no than yes with me, Bill.'

'She'll do as I tell her, Fagin,' said Sikes.

'No, she won't, Fagin,' said Nancy.

'Yes, she will, Fagin,' said Sikes. And he was right. By dint of alternate threats, promises and bribes, the lady in question was ultimately prevailed upon to undertake the task of watching Brownlow's house and finding a way to steal Oliver back. She was dressed in a clean white apron which tied over her gown, and her curls were tucked up under a straw bonnet, both articles of dress being provided from Fagin's inexhaustible stock. Miss Nancy was soon ready to issue forth on her errand.

'Stop a minute, my dear,' said Fagin, producing a little covered basket. 'Carry that in one hand. It looks more respectable.'

'Give her a door key to carry in t'other one, Fagin,' said Sikes. 'It looks real and genuine, like.'

'Yes, yes, so it does,' said Fagin, hanging a large door key on the forefinger of the young lady's right hand. 'There, very good! Very good indeed, my dear!' he said, rubbing his hands. 'Go now and watch Brownlow's home. Discover where the boy sleeps and the movement of the household.' Fagan peered at Nancy. 'Can you do that, my pretty?'

Nancy did a little twirl, clutching her basket close. 'That I can. I look proper enough, I warrant, to stand outside and not cause no suspicion.' She paused and looked at Bill long and hard. 'Before I go, I've got to say something, get it off my chest, like. I love you, Bill. I'd do anything for you, but I ain't about hurtin' no one.' She frowned. 'You're not going to hurt this boy, are you? Because I won't stand for it. I mean it, Bill.'

'We're not going to hurt anyone,' Fagin swiftly reassured her. 'The boy belongs with us. We're just bringing him home.'

'All right then, wish me luck.' Miss Nancy winked to the company, nodded smilingly round and disappeared out of the door.

'Ah, she's a clever girl, my dears,' said Fagin, turning round to Dodge and Charley, shaking his head gravely as if in mute reproach that they had not followed her bright example.

'She's an honour to her sex,' said Sikes, smiting the table with his enormous fist. 'And if she comes back with no news, I'll wring her pretty little neck.'

Chapter XIV

In which we learn more about Oliver's stay at Brownlow's house

Oliver's injuries had healed well over the last three weeks. A long scar at his temple was now the only sign of his trauma. They were happy days, those of Oliver's recovery. Everything was so quiet, and neat, and orderly; everybody so kind and gentle. After the noise and turbulence, the scream of pain in the midst of which he had always lived, his life to this point, he found the silence more disturbing.

One evening, Oliver was sitting talking to Mrs Bedwin when a message came from Brownlow. It said that he would like to see Oliver Twisted in his study if the boy felt well enough.

'Wait here,' Mrs Bedwin said. 'I will fetch you something to wear.' She returned with a blue tunic. 'Mr Brownlow will be pleased to see you in it.'

Oliver placed the tunic over the vest he was wearing, the smooth silk feeling like water on his arms. He looked down and saw a unicorn and dragon stitched into the cloth.

'Tidy your hair as well,' Mrs Bedwin instructed.

Oliver nodded. He was getting quite good at combing his hair. It had been washed and cut for the first time in living memory just a week ago and he now knew what it was like to sleep a night without scratching his scalp raw.

'Dear heart alive!' Mrs Bedwin said. 'I believe he intends to start your apprenticeship tonight. If I had known, I would have given you a lighter dinner. We don't want you vomiting over his library.'

Oliver raised an eyebrow. 'Why would I vomit?' he asked.

Mrs Bedwin laughed. 'Well, he will have much to show you, won't he? I'd imagine that most of it won't be nice. You do understand that he means to train you up into a monster-hunter?'

Oliver gave a start of alarm. 'He said he was a Knight of Nostradamus.'

'He is,' Mrs Bedwin said. 'And that's a fancy name for a monster-hunter.' She looked at him from head to toe with great self-satisfaction. 'You are ready, I think.' she smiled. 'Mr Brownlow is right. There is something special about you.' The old lady reached forward and adjusted Oliver's collar. 'Go on, you'd better run on to the study. He hates to be kept waiting.'

Oliver did as the old lady bade him. Running across the carpeted landing, he tapped at the study door. On Brownlow calling to him to come in, he found himself in a large room, quite full of books, with a window overlooking some pleasant little gardens. There was a table drawn up before the window, at which Brownlow was seated reading.

When he saw Oliver, he pushed the book away from him, and told him to come near the table and sit down.

Oliver complied, marvelling as to where the people could be found to read such a great number of books as seemed to be written to make the world wiser.

'There are a good many books, are there not, my boy?' said Brownlow, observing the curiosity with which Oliver surveyed the shelves that reached from floor to ceiling.

'A great number, sir,' replied Oliver. 'I never saw so many. I only wish I knew how to read.'

'We shall have to teach you how then,' said the old gentleman. 'If you are to learn the art of what it means to be a Knight of Nostradamus.'

'Monster-hunting, you mean?' Oliver said.

Mr Brownlow sighed. 'I suppose Mrs Bedwin has

been chewing off your ears with her talk. The Knights of Nostradamus are protectors and wielders of good magic – we are the only reason this world has not been completely overrun by darkness.'

'So you don't hunt monsters then, sir?' Oliver asked, confused.

'Oh no, we do that. We travel all over the world searching for those places where demons and fiends terrorise the innocent and we do battle.'

Oliver thought about the bloodfarm where he had grown up, and how he and the other children had been fed on day after day. He thought about the workhouse where the Brotherhood of Fenris sacrificed children and ate their corpses. He even thought about Fagin and the boys he kept in his employ, each with a key round his neck, and for the first time Oliver wondered if Dodge and the boys were really there willingly.

Oliver felt a flash of anger and before he could stop the words, he said, 'I don't think the Knights of Nostradamus are picking the right battles.'

One of Brownlow's eyebrows shot up. 'Well I never!'

'I do not mean to be rude, sir,' Oliver said swiftly. 'But my whole life has been blighted by fiends, dark creatures that take advantage of the innocent. If the Knights of Nostradamus were created to protect people like me, then it has not worked.'

Brownlow looked at the boy grimly and Oliver readied himself for the words of banishment that would surely come next.

'Now,' said Brownlow after a moment, 'I want you to pay great attention to what I am going to say. I shall talk to you without any reserve because I am sure you are well able to understand me, as someone far older than yourself would be.'

Oliver nodded. 'I'm ready for you to show me the door. I spoke out of turn.'

Brownlow smiled. 'You spoke exactly as you should have. Never berate yourself for speaking the truth.' His voice dropped an octave. 'The Knights of Nostradamus are under serious threat. Our numbers dwindle every day as dark creatures seek us out and try to destroy us. Many have been slain over these past years and many more have simply fled.' Brownlow rose to his feet and went over to one of the walls lined with books. 'Oliver, I want to show you something. Something I have only ever shown a handful of people.' He took a purple tome from the shelf then the whole bookcase gave a shudder and began to roll back as if invisible hands were pulling it.

It revealed a chamber, walls lined with swords and axes that glinted in the low light. Spears, clubs, bows and arrows were piled on the floor, and glass orbs filled with fire, and others filled with ice, hung from the rafters. Tall staves carved with symbols stood upright in the corners of the room.

'What is this place?' Oliver asked. He turned in a slow circle, his eyes greedily trying to take everything in.

'The Knights' Armoury,' Brownlow replied. 'It holds all the weapons for the London Chapter. We train here and it is the weapons in this room that allow us to fight what demons we can. But you are right – we need to do a better job and, Oliver, I think you can help us do that. You have powerful magic.'

'But, sir, even if that were true. I can't use it.' His fingers crept to the key round his neck.

'Don't worry, Oliver, we will find a way to remove the key. I already have people looking for a solution. No charm is unbreakable. Our time until then will be spent teaching you how to wield weapons of magical attack and defence.'

Brownlow took an axe with an emerald handle off the wall and tossed it at the boy.

Instinctively, Oliver put up a hand and caught it, surprised at how light the axe felt in his grasp.

'That is an Axe of the Darvish. There are not many left in the world. Trust in it and it will guide your blows, and if you have a true affinity with it, it will lend you extra strength.' Brownlow swung round in a fluid, wide arc, plucked a sword from the wall and with no further ado charged at Oliver, his long tunic a blur of blue.

'What are you doing, sir?' Oliver yelled as Brownlow thrust the sword towards him. He jumped back as the tip of the sword grazed his chest.

'I believe it is called testing your mettle, young Oliver,' Brownlow responded. And with a yell he charged forward again, sword held high.

Oliver thrust out with his axe with a returning cry, the edge of the weapon meeting the blade in a shower of sparks. Brownlow slashed out again and again, and for each stroke Oliver met him, whirling and ducking as he brought the axe up to defend himself.

The axe seemed to have a life of its own and it urged him on to fight harder, stronger, fiercer. Oliver felt muscles in his arms that he never knew he had twitching with power as he slashed out and soon he had Brownlow up against the corner of the room. Oliver raised his axe, ready to deliver the final killer blow, but he stopped as he looked at Brownlow, leaning against the wall. The older man was watching him, a smile tugging at his lips.

Oliver let the axe fall to the floor with a clatter, his chest heaving.

'Mr Brownlow, sir, I am so sorry. I don't know what came over me.'

Brownlow pushed up from the wall. 'Nothing to

apologise for.' He rubbed his hands together. 'In fact, I couldn't be more pleased. The axe chimed with you. Oliver, you are a natural Knight.'

'I am?' Oliver questioned. 'I wanted to kill you, sir. I almost did.'

'Tish, tosh. You just got a bit carried away. This type of axe can make that happen sometimes. There is nothing to worry about.' Brownlow adjusted the spectacles on his nose. 'A warrior like you is exactly what we've been looking for. Imagine how powerful you will be when you're free of the cursed key and able to tap into your powers. The Brotherhood will be quaking in their boots.'

'But what if that power is bad magic?' Oliver whispered. 'What if it makes me evil?'

'I should think not,' rejoined the old gentleman. 'It is true I have seen good people turned evil by their abilities, but I have also seen bad turning to good.' Brownlow looked sad. 'I thought the latter was not possible, but I was wrong and I never got to tell that to the one I loved the most dearly in this world.' The old man squared his shoulders, as if shrugging off his grief. 'Oliver, as in all things, it is merely a question of spirit and you have that in spades.' He laughed self-consciously. 'And there is something about your face that reminds me of one I have loved and lost, and so I am more interested in your person than I can well account for, even to myself. So, Oliver, will you join the Knights of Nostradamus?'

Oliver Twisted stood quite still, but then a smile spread across his face. 'If you will have me, sir, I would be happy to become an apprentice of the Knights. I have seen what evil lies out there. I will not let you down.'

'Well, well!' said the old gentleman in a more cheerful tone. 'Then we are the same, you and I. Deep affliction has strengthened our resolve to scour the evil from this land forever and help the innocent.' Brownlow bent down to pick up the axe and placed it on the wall along with his sword. He turned with a thoughtful expression. 'You say you are an orphan, without a friend in the world. All the enquiries I have been able to make confirm the statement, but if you have anything else to tell me, now is the best time.'

Lord Skinim's voice suddenly came to Oliver as loud as a clanging bell. 'He is the key to obliterating the Knights once and for all.' But he could not make himself say it. He could not bear it if Brownlow were to send him away. So he said nothing.

Brownlow slapped a hand on Oliver's shoulder and closed the armoury behind him. 'Come, let me show you some of those books you were so interested in. I will read the text to you and you can learn about the manner of beast you will face in the future.'

Oliver and Brownlow were poring over his collection of books and new methods that detailed how to destroy a vampyre without staking it when a peculiarly impatient little double-knock was heard at the street door. Shortly after, a servant ran upstairs and announced somebody called Grimwig.

'Is he coming up?' enquired Brownlow.

'Yes, sir,' replied the servant. 'He asked if there were any muffins in the house, and when I told him yes, he said he had come to tea.'

Brownlow smiled and, turning to Oliver, told him that Grimwig was also a Knight of Nostradamus. 'I warn you, he is a little rough in his manners, but a worthy creature at bottom, as I have good reason to know.'

'Shall I go downstairs, sir?' enquired Oliver.

'No,' replied Brownlow. 'I would rather you remained here.'

At this moment there walked into the room, supporting himself by a thick cane with the distinctive unicorn and dragon on top, a stout old gentleman, rather lame in one leg. He was dressed in a blue tunic, breeches and a broad-brimmed white hat, with the sides turned up with green; a very long steel chain, with nothing but a dagger at the end, dangled loosely below it. He had a golden torque round his neck, the ends twisted in a shape to defy description. He had a manner of screwing his head on one side when he spoke, and of looking out of the corners of his eyes at the same time, as if he hoped to see behind him as well as in front.

In this attitude, he stared at Oliver, pointed a finger and exclaimed, in a growling, discontented voice, 'Look here! What's that?' The man retreated a pace or two.

'This is young Oliver Twisted, whom we were speaking of some days ago,' Brownlow said.

Oliver bowed.

'You don't mean to say that's the boy who lay sick in one of your beds upstairs, I hope?' said Mr Grimwig, recoiling a little more. 'Wait a minute! Don't speak! Why is he still here? You said he would leave.'

'Don't react so my friend,' said Brownlow, laughing. 'Come! Put down your hat and speak to my young friend. You will see that he is sound.'

Grimwig snorted. 'Brownlow, we spoke of this. You cannot let any waif or stray into your home or through your defences for that matter.' Grimwig banged his cane on the floor. 'How many times must I warn you. This boy might be a spy from the Brotherhood of Fenris, or worse, an assassin. Maybe you would take more notice if I were to eat my own head, sir! Like the good people of Glim.'

Brownlow frowned. 'Grimwig, retract that. Oliver is to be trusted. He has great power. He will be an asset to us.'

'Or our undoing. Brownlow. Only once in all my

years as a Knight have I let down my defences, and I was lamed. I only just escaped with my life. And let us not forget what happened to poor Agnes – she ended up falling in love with that warlock, Leeford.'

Brownlow slammed the table with a fist and his eyes flashed. 'You know better than to say my daughter's name. Have you taken leave of your senses?'

'Have you taken leave of yours?' Grimwig shot back, striking his stick upon the ground again. 'I feel strongly on this subject, sir.' The gentleman drew off his gloves. 'There's always evil and we must be vigilant of it. That boy's an assassin! A mantrap. So he is. I'll prove it.'

Here, the irascible old man drew a monocle from his pocket and took a view of Oliver who, seeing that he was the object of inspection, coloured and felt a tremor go through him.

'Show me the boy's intention,' Grimwig murmured.

Oliver felt the view of the monocle cut through him like a knife through butter and he shuddered again. He knew that he would never mean to hurt Brownlow, but he also knew that the Brotherhood had said that he could be used as a weapon against the Knights. What would the monocle reveal?

Grimwig lowered the eyeglass with a frown. 'How are you, boy?'

'A great deal better, thank you, sir,' replied Oliver,

deciding bravado was the best option. 'Especially now that you are not using your eyeglass. Its gaze is rather painful.'

Brownlow seemed to apprehend that Grimwig was about to say something disagreeable and so swiftly asked, 'What did you see?'

Grimwig looked somewhat sour. 'His patterns are not quite clear, but his intentions seem pure. Still, there is more to this boy than meets the eye. A violent magic lies in his veins.'

'Show him the key, Oliver,' Brownlow instructed.

Oliver did as he was bidden and Grimwig's lips pursed into a thin line as he studied the object.

'Don't you see?' Brownlow said. 'We have to help the boy, free him of this bondage.'

'But where does he come from? Who is he? What is he?' Grimwig asked. 'Perhaps this key was put on him for good reason. When are you going to hear a full, true and particular account of the life and adventures of Oliver Twisted?'

'Tomorrow morning,' replied Brownlow. 'I would rather he were alone with me at the time. Oliver, come up to me tomorrow morning at ten o'clock.'

'Yes, sir,' replied Oliver. He answered with some hesitation, because he was disconcerted by Grimwig looking so hard at him.

'I'll tell you what,' said that gentleman to Brownlow.

'I will bring you my most powerful of spyglasses. It will be able to tell you if Oliver is lying when he answers your questions.'

Brownlow nodded. 'If he is happy to do this, then will you trust him, Grimwig? I want to make the boy an apprentice of the Knights.'

The old man nodded.

'What say you, Oliver?' Brownlow asked.

'I-I –' Oliver could not finish his sentence.

'See him hesitate, Brownlow?' Grimwig crowed triumphantly. 'He is deceiving you, my good friend.'

'I'll swear he is not,' replied Brownlow.

'If he is not,' said Grimwig, 'I'll eat my head!' And down went the stick.

'I'll answer for that boy's truth with my life!' Brownlow said, knocking the table.

'And I for his falsehood with my head!' rejoined Grimwig, knocking the table also. 'Let's see if he is still here tomorrow morning to answer your questions.'

'We shall see.' Brownlow swallowed hard and checked his rising anger.

'We will,' replied Grimwig, with a provoking smile. 'We will.'

As fate would have it, Mrs Bedwin chanced to bring in at this moment a small parcel, and said, 'A delivery from the Paris Chapter of the Knights of Nostradamus.'

She prepared to leave the parlour, but Grimwig stopped her. 'Take the boy, Mrs Bedwin. I do not want him near while we discuss Knights' business.'

Mrs Bedwin frowned at Grimwig, clearly not liking his words or tone, but she led Oliver out of the room.

'Sleep well, Oliver,' Brownlow called after him. 'We will talk tomorrow.'

'Yes sir.' Oliver bowed as he drew the door closed behind him, and sighed as he walked after Mrs Bedwin. He knew that he would have to tell Brownlow about what the Brotherhood had said about him and his powers to destroy the Knights. *He'll never want me for an apprentice then*, he thought. *He'll tell me to leave, or maybe even worse, and I wouldn't blame him.*

He was about to leave Mrs Bedwin and go up the next flight of stairs to his room when he heard someone shout, 'Stop!'

Oliver whipped round to see one of Brownlow's servants on the step of the street door that was wide open. 'Stop!' the servant wailed again.

'Mildred, what in all of heaven do you think you are doing, screaming from the doorway like a low caste banshee?' Mrs Bedwyn berated her. 'You know better than to have the door open like that.'

'Sorry, ma'am.' The young girl clutched a bundle of clothing to her chest. 'But I'm trying to stop that garment tinker to sell him what I've got here. He won't come this way again for another month and I need the extra cash.' The girl looked distraught. 'What should I do?'

'I'll run out and catch him,' Oliver offered.

Mrs Bedwin looked hesitant. 'Mr Brownlow said that you should not go out on any account.'

'Don't worry.' Oliver grabbed the clothes. 'I'll be back before he even notices I'm gone. Promise.'

Oliver ran through the open doorway and after the garment tinker. He hadn't realised how much he missed being outside and drank in the cool night air thirstily. In no time at all, he had caught the tinker and was pleased with the rate he had negotiated before handing over the clothes. In high spirits, he began to walk back. As he did so, he passed a young woman with a clean white apron tied round her waist and a bonnet on her head. She was standing on the street corner under a lamp, tears streaming down her face.

'Excuse me, miss, are you all right?' Oliver asked.

'Oh, my brother! My poor, dear, sweet, innocent little brother!' exclaimed the woman, bursting into fresh sobs and wringing her hands in an agony of distress. 'What will become of him? Where will they take him to? Oh, do have pity, and help me find the dear boy, please.'

'Your brother?' Oliver repeated. 'I have not seen him. Who has taken him?'

'Foul piskies,' the woman replied. 'Stole him from me, they did. I saw them drag him over yonder.' The young woman pointed into a maze of streets off the main thoroughfare. 'Please help me find him.'

Oliver stood a bit straighter. He was an apprentice of the Knights of Nostradamus – it was his duty to help the innocent. 'Of course,' he said. 'Show me the way.'

The girl wiped her face and gave a tremulous smile. 'Thank you, young sir. That is very brave and very kind.'

Oliver felt his chest puff with pride. If he could help this poor girl find her brother, that would prove to Grimwig that he was a good person – it might even convince Brownlow to let him stay, even after he learnt the truth about the Brotherhood and their plans for Oliver.

He thrust out his hand. 'My name is Oliver,' he said.

'And my name is Nancy,' the girl responded.

'Nice to meet you, Nancy. Let us go and find your brother.'

Chapter XV

Showing how important Oliver Twisted was to Fagin and Miss Nancy

At precisely the same time that Oliver agreed to help Nancy find her brother, Bill Sikes was about to get into a fight. He sat brooding in Fagin's dark and gloomy den, where a flaring gaslight burnt all day in the wintertime. Even by that dim light, it was possible to see what a foul mood Sikes was in. At his feet sat the white-coated, red-eyed wolf, who occupied himself by alternately winking at his master with his one eye, and in licking a large, fresh cut on one side of his mouth, which appeared to be the result of some recent conflict. The wolf let out a whine.

'Keep quiet, Bullseye,' said Sikes. 'And quit your complaining. This is where we're stayin'! There's too many people hunting us at the old gaff.'

Bullseye gave a low growl of protest, and his one

eye looked thoroughly aggrieved.

Whether Sikes was feeling especially disgruntled because of his homeless state or whether he just didn't like the tone of Bullseye's growl is matter for argument and consideration. Whatever the cause, the effect was a hard kick and a curse, bestowed upon the wolf simultaneously.

Pets are not generally apt to avenge injuries inflicted upon them by their masters, but Bullseye was more than a pet. He was a brother both in temper and blood, and at once fixed his teeth in one of Sikes's half-boots. Having given it a hearty shake, he retired, growling, just escaping the fist which Sikes levelled at his head.

'You think we are equals, do you?' said Sikes, seizing the poker in one hand and deliberately opening with the other a large clasp-knife, which he drew from his pocket. 'You think you can bite me and that I should bite you back perhaps.' Sikes's hand tightened on the poker. 'You ungrateful cur. Come here, Bullseye, and I'll show you who is master. D'ye hear?'

The wolf no doubt heard because Sikes spoke in the very harshest key of a very harsh voice. But, appearing to entertain some unaccountable objection to having his throat cut, he remained where he was and growled more fiercely than before. Then he leapt up and grasped the end of the poker between his teeth, biting at it.

This resistance only infuriated Sikes the more, who

dropped to his knees and began to assail the animal most furiously. Anger getting the better of him, he began to transform. Thick bristles started to sprout along the man's arms and sharp canines cut through his gums.

Bullseye jumped from right to left, and from left to right, snapping, growling and barking. Sikes thrust and swore, and struck and blasphemed, and the struggle was reaching a most critical point for one or other when the door opened. Bullseye darted out, leaving Bill Sikes with the poker and the clasp-knife in his hands.

There must always be two parties to a quarrel, says the old adage. Sikes, being disappointed of Bullseye's participation, at once transferred his share in the quarrel to the newcomer.

'What the devil do you come in between me and Bullseye for?' said Sikes, with a fierce gesture.

Fagin looked at Sikes, taking in the prominent teeth and the thick bristles that had erupted on his skin. 'I see the wolf has come out to play, Bill,' he said. 'Can I remind you that this is my house.'

Sikes looked down at his arms and then touched one of his canines with a finger. 'Some of the wolf, but not all,' he confessed grudgingly.

'Come, there is news of Twisted,' Fagin said. 'Nancy's observation of the house has finally paid off after these many days. One of my boys saw her leading Oliver on a merry chase. They are close to Clerkenwell.'

'Why'd you need me?' Sikes asked sullenly. 'You are the puppet master. Go and make the boy dance to your tune and bring him back here.'

'Twisted is reputed to have much power,' Fagin wheedled. 'My control through the key might not work.'

'Not work!' Sikes sneered. 'I've never heard such nonsense.'

Fagin felt a flash of pride at the backhanded compliment. 'It is true my ability to control others cannot be rivalled. But it cannot hurt to have someone of your particular abilities by my side.' Fagin made what he hoped was a humble face.

The real truth, of course, was that he was worried a Knight of Nostradamus might be close by and Sikes would be a good shield to have.

'Oh no, old man,' said Sikes, replacing the poker, and surveying him with savage contempt. 'You'll never outwit me. I've got the upper hand over you, Fagin, and I'll keep it. I'll go with you, but take heed of what I say.'

'I know all that,' Fagin said. 'We have a mutual interest, Bill, a mutual interest.'

'Humph,' said Sikes. 'Come, let's collect the boy and then we can collect our reward.'

'About that . . .' Fagin began.

Sikes banged a fist on the table. 'Well, what have you got to say to me?'

'Our reward will come to us soon enough, but we will have to be patient. I spoke to Lord Skinim this morning. I have disguised the fact that Oliver has been with Brownlow these past weeks, but they have asked how his corruption is progressing. They will not pay until they see some results and soon.'

'Wolfsbane!' swore Sikes impatiently. 'How will you corrupt the boy? He's bound to have the stink of the Knights on him.'

Fagin tapped the side of his nose. 'I have my ways, but we have to catch him first.'

'Then let us go and pick up the boy's scent,' Sikes growled. He strode out of the door followed by Fagin. Bullseye, who had been watching from a corner outside the door, waited until he thought no one was looking and then slunk out close behind them.

Not so far away, Oliver Twisted was busy on the fool's errand of trying to help Nancy find her little brother.

'Are you sure it's down here?' Oliver peered into a dark alleyway.

Nancy looked into the passage as well and nodded. 'It is exactly the kind of place the piskies would choose,' she said.

They turned down the alley, the light leaving them as they got halfway down it. At the other end Oliver could hear a howling noise and the sound made the hairs on his arms stand on end.

'I am not sure this is the right direction, Nancy. We should turn back.'

'Just a little further,' Nancy begged. 'He could be down there.'

'What is your brother's name?' Oliver asked. 'I should have asked before.'

Nancy bit her lip. 'His name . . .' she said, her eyes darting from side to side. 'His name, his name.'

Oliver turned to face Nancy, the unease he had felt at the howl now becoming full-blown alarm as the girl struggled to produce an answer.

Suddenly there was a streak of fur and a wolf with a vicious scar across its face darted forward. Oliver saw a flash of teeth as the wolf latched on to his calf. He cried out and shook his leg to try and free himself. He had barely kicked off the wolf when a pair of arms were thrown tight round his neck.

'Stop!' cried Oliver, trying to fight to get free. 'Let go of me.'

The only reply to this was a growl and Oliver turned his head to see a cheek shadowed by whiskers and an eye that looked bloodshot and fierce. The wolf that stood nearby growled as well and, licking his lips, eyed Oliver as if he were anxious to attach himself to his windpipe without delay.

'Nancy, run!' Oliver cried. But Nancy didn't move, her eyes wide and guilty. Oliver felt his stomach clench as he realised that a snare had been set and he was the hare.

'Who are you? Let me go,' cried Oliver. He tried to wrench himself from the man's powerful grasp, but his arm was twisted viciously. Oliver gave a gasp of pain. 'Nancy, help me, please.'

'I – I'm sorry, I can't,' Nancy said, her voice full of regret.

'Hold him tight, Bill.' A familiar voice came from the shadows. 'He is a slippery one.'

Oliver struggled even more furiously as the hunched figure of Fagin stepped towards him.

'Stop your fussing now, young Oliver,' Fagin soothed. 'Stop your fighting.'

Oliver felt the key around his neck go very cold. Ice spread his through limbs and made them heavy and stiff. He fought against the feeling – every thought, every breath screaming with resistance.

Fagin expelled a pained sigh. 'You are not easy, boy, not easy at all.' The old man straightened his shoulders. 'Stop struggling,' he commanded and he passed a hand across Oliver's forehead.

Oliver's legs stopped kicking, his arms stilled.

'That's it, boy,' Fagin said. 'Now close your eyes and sleep.'

Despite himself, Oliver's eyelids began to droop and the last thing he saw was Nancy's worried face and the little basket that hung from her arm.

Back at Brownlow's house, the gaslamps were lighted and Mrs Bedwin was waiting anxiously at the open door. The servant girl had run up the street twenty times to see if there were any traces of Oliver.

Brownlow sat in the dark parlour, his heart heavy, knowing that Grimwig had been right. Oliver had not been all that he seemed and, with the threat of having his true self revealed, he had fled. 'It is better he is gone, before any more damage could be done,' Brownlow said to the empty room. *So why do I feel so sad?*

Chapter XVI

Relates what became of Oliver Twisted,
after he had been reclaimed by Fagin

The night was dark and foggy. The lights in the shops could scarcely struggle through the heavy mist, which thickened every moment and shrouded the streets and houses in gloom, rendering the strange place still stranger to Oliver's half-closed eyes.

Fagin, Nancy and Sikes – with the burden of Oliver over his shoulder – hurried on a few paces, when a deep church bell struck the hour. With its first stroke, Fagin and Nancy stopped, and turned their heads in the direction whence the sound proceeded.

'Eight o'clock,' said Nancy, when the bell ceased.

'What's the good of telling me that? I can hear it, can't I!' replied Sikes, who still strode ahead.

The girl burst into a laugh and drew her shawl more closely round her. 'We should take another route back,' she said, looking fearfully at the silhouette of the gallows that were a little distance ahead of them. 'There was a hanging today, there's bound to be wisps.'

'Let them come,' Sikes growled. 'I'm not scared of them.'

'You should be, Fagin murmured. 'I've seen wisps do terrible things. They are incredibly powerful. Mindless, they are, just a ball of hate.'

'And wouldn't you be full of hate as well,' Nancy shot back, 'if you were killed before your time?' She nodded at the gallows. 'Most of those hanged here were innocent of any crime.'

'I've never seen one before,' Sikes admitted. 'But I've heard them. Me and my mate Toby Crackit were locked up for the night. We could hear the row and din outside our jail door. The sound of skulls being crushed on the iron plates as the wisps beat out the brains of the guards that had led them to the gallows that very morning.'

'So why aren't you scared, Bill?' Nancy asked, clutching her shawl even closer. 'You know what a wisp can do.'

'But I ain't done them hanged today any wrong,' Sikes replied. 'They'll have scores to settle elsewhere.'

'Well, I am not as sure as you, Bill,' Fagin said. 'And I'd prefer not to run into a wisp. Come on, let's get the boy home.'

They walked on, veering away from the gallows. At length they turned into a very filthy, narrow street, full of old apothecary shops; Bullseye, running forward as if conscious that there was no further occasion for his keeping on guard, stopped before the door of Fagin's house. It was in a ruinous condition. On the door was nailed a board, intimating that plague and pestilence lay within. It looked as if it had hung there for many years.

'All right,' cried Sikes, glancing cautiously about.

Nancy and Fagin stooped below the shutters and Oliver heard the sound of a bell. They crossed to the opposite side of the street and stood for a few moments under a lamp. A noise was heard, as if a sash window were gently being raised, and soon afterwards the door softly opened.

'Ankou's thief,' Fagin said.

Sikes then stalked through the door, Oliver still on his shoulder, and all four were quickly inside the house. The passage was perfectly dark. They waited while the person who had let them in chained and barred the door.

'Who is here?' enquired Fagin.

'Me and Charley,' Dodge's voice replied.

'Let's have a light,' said Sikes, 'or we shall go breaking our necks, or treading on Bullseye, and he would not like that!'

'Stand still a moment and I'll get you one,' replied the boy. The receding footsteps of the speaker were heard and, in another minute, the form of Dodge appeared. He bore in his right hand a tallow candle stuck in the end of a cleft stick.

'What've you done to him then?' Dodge pointed at Oliver.

'He's just getting a bit of rest,' Fagin chuckled. 'Albeit against his will.'

The young gentleman nodded and did not stop to look on Oliver again, but turning away headed up a flight of stairs, the others following him. They crossed an empty kitchen and opened the door of a low, earthy-smelling room, which seemed to have been built in a small backyard. They were received with a shout of laughter.

'Oh, my!' cried Charley Bates, from whose lungs the laughter had proceeded. 'Here he is! Oh, Fagin, look at his togs.' Charley put the light so close to Oliver's new tunic as nearly to set him on fire. 'Superfine cloth and the emblem of the Knights sewn on his breast! Fagin, do look at him, a true Knight of Nostradamus! I can't bear it. Hold me, somebody, while I laugh it out.'

With this irrepressible ebullition of mirth, Charley laid himself flat on the floor and kicked convulsively for five minutes, in an ecstasy of facetious joy.

Dodge picked up the candle that Charley was about to knock over. 'Give over, will you?' he said. 'We've got him back now, no need to go on.'

Charley jumped to his feet. 'And why are you so precious of his feelings? He warned Brownlow and almost got you caught.'

Dodge shrugged. 'Oliver saved my life. I can't forget that.' He flicked the brim of his hat. 'After Oliver saw off those woe-begottens, I told him that he could trust me, but he couldn't. So he may have betrayed me, but I betrayed him first.'

'How noble and philosophical of you, Dodge,' Fagin sneered. 'But you're sounding soft to me and I don't like it.' He yanked at the key round Dodge's throat. 'Snap out of it or I will snap you.'

'Yes, Fagin,' Dodge muttered.

'Good. Lie the boy down,' the soul-stealer ordered.

Oliver opened one eye as he was lowered to the floor. He had been awake through the whole conversation, as painful as it had been not to react. The key was no longer freezing and the weight in his limbs, that had made them seem immovable before, had disappeared. Oliver realised that even the fact he could open his eyes meant that Fagin was no longer concentrating on keeping him asleep.

Taking a deep breath, he jumped to his feet and tore wildly from the room.

'Fagin, stop him!' Sikes roared so loudly that he made the bare old house echo to the roof.

Oliver reached the door before he felt Fagin's control begin to seep into him from the key. The metal was so cold it almost felt like a flame burning away his free will. Oliver fought against it, his fingers scrambling to find the door handle. He managed to wrench the door open and spilt out on to the landing.

Behind him he could hear the excited yelping of the wolf and then the rip of clothing and the low howl of another. Oliver pelted off down the hallway and leapt over the stair bannister, landing in a crouch. His heart was pounding with both fear and elation. The further he got away from Fagin the less he could feel his control. *I'll make it*, he thought. *If I can just get out of the house.*

Back in the parlour, Nancy had thrown herself in front of the door that Fagin, Charley and Dodge had just darted out of in pursuit of Oliver. 'Keep in the wolf, Bill!' cried Nancy, slamming the door shut. 'Keep in the wolf or you'll tear the boy to pieces. I told you I'd help you find the boy, but I ain't about hurting no one. I said that.'

Bullseye was now howling furiously, standing with Bill as he faced Nancy.

'Serve him right!' cried Sikes, his voice somewhere between a snarl and a sneer. 'Move away from that door or I'll split your head against the wall.'

'I don't care for that, Bill, I don't care for that,' screamed the girl, refusing to cower as the wolfman stalked towards her. 'The child shan't be torn down by you, unless you kill me first.'

'Shan't he!' said Sikes, baring his teeth. 'I'll soon do that, if you don't move.'

The wolfman sprang forward and grabbed Nancy, his claws sinking into the softness of her arm, tearing the skin. A scream of agony left her mouth and he flung her to the further end of the room.

Just then, the door swung open and Fagin and the two boys returned. They were dragging Oliver between them, his body as stiff as a board.

'What's the row here!' said Fagin looking around. 'Oh Bill, there was no need to bring out the wolf, we had it all under control. Dodge here turned to smoke and caught young Oliver by the door.' Fagin shook his head. 'Look at all this blood. You've got it on my drapes.'

'What have you done to Nancy?' Dodge demanded, his face thunderous.

'The girl's gone mad, I think,' growled Sikes. He rose up on two legs once more, his clothes rags around him.

There was a wet slurping sound as his muzzle sank back into his face and his jaw shortened, the savage canines retracting. With a hiss, the thick bristles on his arms and face slipped back into open follicles which eagerly closed over them.

'No, she hasn't.' Nancy was on her feet, pale from the loss of blood. Her hand was clamped over the wound on her arm, scarlet seeped from between her fingers. 'No, she hasn't, Fagin, don't think it.'

'If you ain't mad, keep quiet, will you?' said Fagin, with a worried look. 'You'll just make him turn again.'

'No, I will not keep quiet neither,' replied Nancy, speaking very loud. 'Come! What do you think of that?'

Fagin was sufficiently well acquainted with the manners and customs of Nancy to feel tolerably certain that it would be rather unsafe to prolong any conversation with her at present. With the view of diverting the attention of the company, he turned to Oliver.

'So you wanted to get away, did you?' he said with a glare. 'Eh?'

Oliver made no reply. His body was still completely stiff, paralysed by Fagin's control. He watched Fagin as the old man approached, the sound of his own breathing filling his head.

'Wanted to get assistance, call for the Knights, did

171

you?' sneered Fagin, catching the boy by the arm.

'Yes,' Oliver railed back. 'The Knights are worth ten of you. They are good and fair, smart, strong. Everything you're not.'

Fagin's face went into spasm as Oliver spoke these words.

Sikes guffawed with laughter. 'Well, the boy told you, old man.'

Fagin's lips pressed so thin that an edge of white rimmed them. 'You dare to praise them?' he cried, taking up a jagged and knotted club which lay in a corner of the fireplace. 'Do you know what they did to me, to my kind?' The old man inflicted a smart blow across Oliver's face with the weapon. 'They hunted us, killed us.'

Oliver felt the plumpness of his lip split, and a tooth clattered to the floor. Blood ran freely down his chin, but he could not even raise a hand to stop it.

Behind Fagin's shoulder, Oliver could see Dodge and Charley watching. As usual Charley had a stupid grin plastered on his face, but Dodge . . . well, Dodge's face was filled with anger.

Fagin raised his club a second time.

'Stop, Fagin,' Dodge said. 'That's enough.'

Fagin whipped round and glared at the dodger. 'I'll split that smart mouth of yours as well, if you don't shut up.' And with a flick of his finger, he made Dodge slap a hand over his mouth.

Fagin faced Oliver and raised his club again when Nancy rushed forward and wrested it from his hand. She flung it into the fire, with a force that brought some of the glowing coals whirling out into the room.

'I won't stand by and see it done, Fagin,' cried the girl. 'You've got the boy, and what more would you have? Let him be, let him be, or I shall put the mark on you.'

Fagin laughed. 'The mark? You don't have that power.'

Sikes gave a snort of agreement. 'You're a barmaid, Nancy, and other things besides, but you are not a witch. Now sit down.'

The girl stamped her foot violently on the floor, her lips compressed and her palms clenched. Blood ran in a tide down her arm from the wound the wolfman had given her, and the hand that she held up was covered in red. With crooked fingers, she pointed at Sikes and then Fagin. 'I curse you,' she whispered. 'And for each day that comes, may it be filled with the pain and hurt you have inflicted on others. May you end your days alone and afraid. May you be served a dish of your own making.' Nancy's face was quite colourless now and blood puddled on the floor, soaking her shoes.

'Why, Nancy!' said Fagin in a soothing tone, after

a pause, during which he and Sikes had stared at one another in a disconcerted manner. 'You're more impressive than ever tonight. Ha ha, my dear! You haven't really put the mark on us, have you?'

'Aye, I have,' said the girl. 'Take care I don't do it again and bring your demise even sooner. You will be the worse for it, Fagin, if I do, and so I tell you in good time to keep clear of me.'

Fagin saw that it would be madness to affect any furtherance of the reality of Miss Nancy's curse and, shrinking involuntarily back a few paces, he cast a glance, half imploring and half cowardly, at Sikes, as if to hint that he was the fittest person to fix the situation.

'What do you mean by this, Nancy?' Sikes asked. 'Curse me, will you? You said you loved me.'

'I do, more than you can ever know!' replied the girl, shaking her head from side to side. 'But I've cursed you and I won't take it back.'

'Yes, you will,' rejoined Sikes with a growl. Thick bristles on his arms began to sprout once more. 'Or I'll quiet you for a good long time to come.'

Nancy laughed hysterically. 'Kill me then,' she cried out. 'I wish I had been struck dead in the street before I lent a hand in bringing that innocent boy here. He will be made a devil, all that's bad, from this night forth. Isn't that enough without blows?'

'I shall do you a mischief!' interposed Fagin, goaded by these reproaches. 'A mischief worse than that, if you say much more!'

The girl rushed at Fagin and would have probably left marks of her revenge upon him had not her wrists been seized by Sikes. She gasped in pain, her arm spurted another plume of blood and she fainted.

'Charley, get something to bind her arm,' Sikes said, laying her down in a corner. He nuzzled at her wounded arm. 'She's lost a lot of blood.' He looked at her with something akin to affection. 'My Nancy . . . so full of fire.'

Fagin wiped his forehead. 'Your Nancy may well have put a curse on us.' He touched his throat as if to check that he still had a pulse. 'Impossible to tell if she really has the gift.'

Sikes shook his head. 'She was just trying to frighten you, Fagin. Pay her no mind.'

The old man nodded. 'Dodge, put Oliver to bed.'

Dodge mumbled something in reply, but could not be understood because of the hand that was still stuck over his mouth. Fagin laughed. 'Of course, I forgot.' He flicked a finger and Dodge lowered his hand.

'What were you trying to say, my boy?'

Dodge looked furious. 'I was trying to say how do you expect me to move him with only one bleedin' hand free.'

Fagin gave another chortle of laughter. 'Well, all solved now.'

Charley came back into the room. 'I can't find nothin' for Nancy's arm.'

A growl rumbled in Sikes chest. 'Fool boy, are you telling me there is nothing suitable in this pit you call a home?'

'There is no need to insult my abode,' Fagin snapped. 'But I understand that you are distraught by the health of dear Nancy and so I will choose to ignore it this time.'

'Well, we can't just stand around,' Dodge said. 'We need to bind her arm and quickly.'

Fagin tapped his chin thoughtfully. 'Don't worry. I have something you can use.' He stepped forward and grabbed the front of Oliver's tunic. With one swift movement, he ripped a wide strip off it.

Oliver's eyes stung as he saw the emblem of the dragon and unicorn dangling in Fagin's hand. He'd had his lip split, a tooth dashed out of his head and his body was no longer his to control, but none of these things pained him as much as seeing the symbol of the Knights so abused.

'Use this rag.' Fagin thrust the material at Sikes. 'Dodge and Charley, make sure you burn the rest of what Oliver is wearing once he is put to bed. I do not want that filth in my house.'

Charley Bates nodded and, helping Dodge, dragged Oliver into an adjacent room, where there were two or three beds.

'Time to get rid of your tunic, mate,' Dodge said.

Although it took almost all of his strength, Oliver managed to shake his head. Dodge's eyes widened in surprise. 'How do you do that?' he murmured. 'I've never been able to resist Fagin's hold, no matter how hard I've tried.'

'FAGIN!' Charley bawled. 'Oliver won't take the tunic off.'

There was the scrape of a chair and Fagin stalked into the room. 'Really, boy, this is becoming most tiresome. Rip that tunic off. Do it right now.'

Oliver unwillingly complied, a cry of rage crawling up his throat as he tore the tunic into shreds and threw them to the floor.

'Now get to sleep,' Fagin commanded. Oliver did as he was told and walked stiffly over to the bed. 'That's more like it. Look at how well we are getting on now.' Fagin gave a cackle before leaving.

Charley, with uncontrollable bursts of laughter, produced an old shirt for Oliver to wear in the morning and draped it over a chair. Dodge knelt down and picked up the scraps of the tunic, then departed from the room alongside Charley. They locked the door behind them.

Oliver was left in the dark, his body still as rigid as a board. His only company was the knowledge that there was no way he could escape Fagin or his gang.

Chapter XVII

A short but important chapter where Oliver is prevailed upon to find his Dark Side

When Oliver awoke in the morning, he found that he could move his body once more, but he quickly wished that he hadn't. Every part of him ached. His head throbbed and with his tongue he probed the socket where a tooth once sat.

'I'm sorry about that, Oliver,' a voice said to his left.

Oliver turned to see Fagin sitting by the bed. 'I shouldn't have lost my temper, but to be fair, you baited me with all that talk of the Knights.' Fagin rubbed at his wrinkled forehead. 'Let us start again. We might as well, for you will be stopping here awhile.'

Oliver sat up in bed. 'You are not going to give me to the Brotherhood then?'

'You know about that, do you?' Fagin shrugged. 'I guess it doesn't matter. They want you to stay with me for a while and I would like that too. So would my boys.'

'They aren't your boys,' Oliver muttered, tugging on the key that hung from his neck. 'They're your prisoners, just like me.'

Fagin folded his arms. 'I hardly ever use the key. They stay with me because we are family. And the same will be true of you once we have finished your induction.'

'Induction?'

'Or perhaps immersion is a better word,' Fagin mused. He revealed the Tablet of Horus from the folds of his dirty coat.

Oliver's eyes widened. He remembered the tablet well from when Fagin had used it to contact Lord Skinim.

'The tablet can do many things,' Fagin murmured reverently. 'But its most useful power is to show a person the true nature of themselves. It will fill this whole room with the truth about you, Oliver. The self you would seek to hide from everyone.' He patted Oliver's head. 'Soon enough, it will be just you and the truth and you will stay in this room for as long as it takes to make you accept it. And after it is all done, after your eyes are so sore they will weep blood, you will come to me and beg to be part of my family because you know that no one else would want you.'

'Never,' Oliver vowed.

'You're a bad 'un, Oliver. I know it, the Brotherhood know it and you'll know it soon enough.'

Fagin whispered an incantation to the tablet and placed in on a shelf. 'Make sure you don't touch it, Oliver. If disturbed, the tablet might trap you in the visions that it is showing you.' He crossed the room to the door but stopped to look over his shoulder. 'Don't be afraid. You shall come back to us better and badder. Ha ha ha! You'll be so cruel, my dear. I can hardly wait.'

The old man shut the door behind him and turned the key in the lock. He smiled as he heard Oliver begin to scream.

Scarcely had the door closed when the room began to change around Oliver, the walls closing in on him. He leapt out of the bed and ran for the door, but however fast he ran, the door always seemed further away.

A shower of dust rained down on him as hands, mottled and grey, suddenly thrust out from the wall and grabbed at him. Fingers raked his face and pulled at his exposed skin. The moan of woe-begottens filled the room and more hands pushed out of the floor.

Oliver closed his eyes. He tried to tell himself it was all just an illusion, Fagin's magic trying to turn him evil, but he could not keep his eyes closed. He had to see what was in front of him. A pack of woe-begottens stood watching him and Oliver immediately recognised them as the same poor, cursed souls he had released in the graveyard.

He backed away from them, his shoulders up against brick. 'W-what are you doing here?' he stammered. 'I set you free. I gave you peace.'

The girl in the tattered dress staggered forward. 'Set us free? You killed us. Took away the only life we had left.'

'No, you wanted peace. I gave you that,' Oliver hurled back.

The woe-begotten was standing right in front of him, her breath a perfume of decay which drowned him. She brought her face right up to Oliver's and he could see the deep yellow of her eyes, the oozing sores on her cheeks which wept freely with pus. 'You killed us, Oliver. You killed us because you are bad.'

'No,' Oliver snarled. He pushed the girl away as she reached for him. She dropped to the ground, her body instantly shattering to pieces.

Oliver began to tremble as he watched her head spin across the floor. 'I'm sorry,' he said. 'I didn't mean it.'

'Too late for sorry,' the girl's head spoke as it rolled. 'Too late for I didn't mean it.'

The pack of woe-begottens crouched to the floor and gathered up the broken pieces of the girl. They held them to their chests, cradling the fractured limbs like newborn babies, their moans now wails of distress.

Oliver could not stand the sound. He ran to the door and battered the wood with his fist. 'I need to get out,' he begged. 'Please.' He tried the handle, but it would not turn.

'Help us?' voices chimed from behind.

Oliver whirled round, expecting to see the woe-begottens, but they had gone and in their place sat rows and rows of boys from the workhouse, each with a bowl in front from which they ate greedily.

When Oliver had last been at the workhouse, the scratchy grey uniform that the boys had been forced to wear had hung loosely from their bodies, and sunken eyes had viewed the thin gruel in their bowls. These boys were wearing clothes that were too tight for them and the skin on their faces was shiny, pink and plump.

'They started feeding you,' Oliver said, relief surging through him.

'You helped us.' The children looked up and spoke as one. 'You got us gore.'

With a cackle, one of the boys upturned his bowl and the wetness of guts and eyeballs flooded across the table. 'See?' the boy said.

'No,' Oliver protested. 'I asked for more.'

'But it was not enough,' they said. 'Never enough. And you went away.'

'I'm sorry,' Oliver said. 'I had no choice.'

'You left us,' the children intoned. 'And now our bellies are full and our souls as dark as tar.'

'I'll get you help,' Oliver vowed. 'Brownlow will save you.'

'Too late, Oliver. Too late for you or us. We need gore, always.' The boys leapt from their benches and began to circle each other, their bodies hunched and their legs bent ready to spring.

'Wait, what are you doing,' Oliver asked, stepping towards them.

'Eat or be eaten,' one boy murmured.

'Eat or be eaten.' The call was taken up by them all. 'EAT OR BE EATEN!!!' The chant was a deafening cry now as savage grins twisted the boys' faces.

'No, no, don't do it!' Oliver screamed. He tried to run towards them, but it felt like his legs were made of stone.

There was a roar and the boys fell on each other. Material tore, hair ripped, blood spilt as they grappled. It didn't take long for the strongest and the wiliest boys to gain the upper hand.

'Stop,' Oliver cried. 'Please.'

In reply, the victims cried out for mercy, while the victors said nothing at all. Teeth were bared as they bit down. They feasted and gobbled, pulling strips off limbs.

'I said stop!' Oliver demanded.

The boys in front of him began to scream as flames appeared at their feet and licked their tattered shoes. Fingers of smoke stretched across the room and took hold. The feasting had stopped, but not the screams as the fire spread.

'What's happening?' Oliver asked in a whisper.

'It's you, Oliver,' one boy said. He whirled in a ball of light, flames becoming hair. 'It's you doing this. It's your fire within. Your Rage, your evil.'

Smoke had filled the whole room now and enveloped the cannibal boys. Oliver began to cough, his breaths becoming short and shallow.

'My evil,' he repeated, collapsing to the floor. His eyes closed. 'Yes, my evil.'

Chapter XVIII

Where Oliver is somewhat changed and the Plan is set afoot

'How's the boy doing then?' Sikes asked.

'The screaming stopped shortly after midnight,' Fagin said. 'Thankfully. I thought I'd get no sleep at all.'

Nancy jumped up from where she sat, appalled at the callous words. 'You're a nasty piece of work, Fagin.'

'I am a genius, dear Nancy. By the end of this day, Oliver will be completely broken.'

'What have you done to him?' Sikes asked.

'I have left him with the Tablet of Horus. I have instructed it to show Oliver his deepest fears – to bring them to life even.' Fagin laughed. 'Poor boy thinks the tablet is showing him his true nature!'

Nancy gasped. 'Do you mean to turn the boy mad?' she asked, cradling her injured arm.

'No, my dear, but the Brotherhood need to see results,' Fagin replied. 'If Oliver believes he is evil, truly evil, he will stop fighting so hard to be good.' The old man smiled. 'He will be clay for the Brotherhood to mould into their perfect weapon, but more importantly, before that we will be able to use him to get to Brownlow and the Knights of Nostradamus.'

'And how is that?' Sikes asked.

'I've been thinking long and hard about it,' Fagin explained. 'Many have said that the Knights' Armoury is in Brownlow's house. I'm sure Oliver could show us where it is hidden and if we were to steal the weapons, well . . .'

Sikes smiled. 'The Knights would be paralysed once and for all.' His eyes glinted. 'We'd be heroes, treated like kings.'

'Bill, to destroy the Knights would be a sweet revenge, but it is only part of the meal. When you get into the house, bring me one of Brownlow's handkerchiefs, then my revenge will be complete.' Fagin rubbed his hands together. 'How it will gladden my heart to eat that man's soul.'

'What are we waiting for then? Let us get the boy and make our plan,' Sikes barked.

'Oliver is still . . . ripening, so to speak,' Fagin explained patiently. 'He will let us know when he is rea –'

Fagin was interrupted by a low, steady knock from the other side of the kitchen door. 'Ha ha,' he said. 'I think our little egg has hatched.' He shuffled over to the door and put his ear to the wood. 'What is it, Oliver?' he asked.

'Let me out of this room,' Oliver said. 'The tablet has nothing left to show me.'

'Hold your horses, Oliver. Are you sure there will be no more crying or talk of what it means to be good?'

'Let me out of this room, right now,' Oliver demanded. 'I tire of your idle chat, you wrinkled old buzzard.'

Fagin raised an eyebrow and looked back at Sikes and Nancy. 'Well, he does not sound much like the old Oliver,' he said.

'Let him out, Fagin. We will soon see his transformation,' Sikes replied.

Fagin nodded and took a bunch of keys from the folds of his filthy dressing gown. He flicked through them until he found the right one and slotted it into the lock and turned it. The door swung open and Oliver crossed the threshold. His face was as white as chalk and his eyes were sunk in his head, so much deeper than any other person's. His cheekbones jutted out like blades over hollow cheeks. Lank hair straggled on to his forehead and his eyelashes were clumped with blood, the whites of his eyes shot through with red.

Nancy gasped. 'Oh. Oliver!' She covered her mouth to muffle a sob.

Oliver turned to look at her and his lips, which were discoloured and disfigured with the marks of teeth, pulled into a sneer. 'Don't like what you see, Nancy?'

'No – I –' Nancy sounded flustered. 'You just look so different, that's all.'

Oliver laughed and it sounded like the creak of a rotten gate. 'I have lived a nightmare,' he whispered. 'And I have become one.'

''Tis good to hear such cheering talk.' Fagin slapped a hand on Oliver's shoulder and guided him to the table. 'Come, let's celebrate your metamorphosis.' The old man brought forth a plate. 'Go on, eat something. A boy cannot live on hate alone.'

'Can he not?' Oliver questioned. 'I find myself without appetite for food, but with other impulses that I seek to feed.' He could hear the echo of the children screaming in the workhouse as the fire overtook them, and the sound was like a soothing brook. He looked at Fagin stonily. 'When will you remove this key? My magic is mine to wield, mine to hurt with.'

'All in good time, Oliver,' Fagin soothed. 'We need to see that you can be trusted.'

Oliver rose slowly to his feet and leant forward so that he was nose to nose with Fagin. 'Trusted?' Oliver hissed. 'You have ripped anything good from me, left only the rotting carcass of hate.' His hand shot out and squeezed Fagin's windpipe, feeling joy course through him and fill the hollowness that was his inside. 'Perhaps if I snap your neck, your control will be snapped as well and then we will not have to wait for you to TRUST.'

Fagin simply gurgled in reply, unable to issue the command for Oliver to stop. His eyes bulged in his head.

Oliver clenched his hand, feeling the delicate bone give just a little under his grip. Sikes, who had been rather occupied by laughing at Fagin's predicament, eased out of his chair and loomed over Oliver.

'Let him go, boy,' Sikes said in an even tone. 'I cannot let you kill him, as much as it pains me to say it.'

Oliver looked up at Sikes. Hate had made him dead inside, but not stupid. He released the soul-stealer, who fell spluttering to the floor.

Fagin rubbed at his throat and glared at Oliver. 'Is that the thanks I get for showing you your true nature?' He gave a rasping cough. 'Well, I needn't have bothered.'

'Tell me what I need to do to get rid of this key round my neck.' Oliver's voice was cold.

'Get us into Brownlow's house and into the Knights' Armoury,' Sikes said.

'It is impossible,' Oliver replied. 'The house is completely protected against attacks from dark agents.

Not even Dodge could slip through a gap.'

'Let me worry about that, boy.' Sikes said. 'My friend Toby Crackit has returned from the New World I heard – he is the best housebreaker I know. He'll find a way through the charms.'

Fagin looked somewhat dubious, but did not dare challenge Sikes – his throat was far too bruised to contemplate another confrontation. 'Once you are in, show Bill to the armoury,' he said instead. 'I warrant you know where it is.'

Oliver nodded once. 'Brownlow took me in there. When do we go?'

'All in good time,' Fagin replied. 'We must prepare first. If that stupid man Brownlow showed you the weapons, then we should start with ascertaining what is in the armoury. I know only rumour and hearsay.'

'He did not give me the name of each weapon,' Oliver said irritably. 'Only the Axe of the Darvish.'

Fagin's eyes widened. 'They have an Axe of the Darvish?' He rubbed his hands gleefully. 'That alone is a prize of kings. What a haul. What a haul this will be.' He crossed his arms upon his breast and, drawing his head into his shoulders, literally hugged himself for joy.

'Get down your book, Fagin,' Sikes ordered. 'Let the boy show us what the Knights have.'

Fagin shuffled over to the fire and reached up to the

shelf that sat above it. He brought down a heavy book covered in the hairy hide of a satyr.

'This book is a complete compendium of the most powerful weapons of our world. It also documents the men, demons and warlocks that have won and lost these magical prizes.'

'Have a look,' Sikes urged. 'And show us the weapons that you have seen.'

Oliver took the book in his hand, stroking the stretched skin beneath his fingertips. As he opened it and looked at the pages, he found himself remembering the time spent in Brownlow's library and the man's promise that he would teach Oliver to read. The boy felt something strange twist in his gut and it took a moment for him to realise that the feeling was guilt. He dismissed it immediately. Guilt belonged to the distant echo of Oliver, not the blood and bone of his new self.

'I cannot read,' he muttered. 'How do you expect me to identify the weapons?'

Nancy here is a fine reader and can call the descriptions out to you, help you make a list,' Fagin explained. 'Sikes and I will start on our plan, but first off we will need Crackit.'

'I'll send one of the boys to get him,' said Sikes, and he and Fagin left the room, leaving Oliver and Nancy alone.

Oliver began flicking through the pages, violently at first, angry that the words in front of him were just a sea of symbols he didn't understand. He stopped as he lighted upon a line drawing of an axe with an emerald set in its handle. His fingers traced the image.

Nancy, who had been hovering nearby hesitantly, looked over his shoulder. 'The description says that this is an Axe of the Darvish.'

'I know what it is,' Oliver snapped. 'Brownlow showed me how to fight with it.'

'Did Brownlow teach you a lot of things then?' Nancy asked, coming to sit next to him. 'Is he a good man?'

'He has a cause that drives him to get rid of evil,' Oliver replied. 'I warrant destroying evil makes him good, so he is good.'

'Are you evil now then?' Nancy whispered.

'I am what I was born to be,' Oliver replied.

'And what is that?'

'A warlock,' he said flatly. 'Dodge called me that when we first met, but I didn't know what that really meant until now.'

Nancy pointed to a passage in the book. 'This also talks of warlocks.'

Oliver peered down at the page, his pale face set into a frustrated frown. 'What does it say?'

'It talks of how rare warlocks are and their affinity

with certain weapons.' Nancy's eyes skimmed the pages, which were soiled and well thumbed with use and began to read out loud.

'The name warlock means oathbreaker or deceiver and they are one of the most powerful races on earth.'

Oliver gave her a stony stare. 'Tell me something I don't know, Nancy. I begin to tire of your squawking voice.' The boy shook his head. 'I wonder how Sikes stands it.'

Nancy took a sharp inhalation of breath at his cruel words. The kind boy who had offered to help a weeping girl find her missing brother had truly gone. She swallowed the lump in her throat made of sadness and guilt and continued to read out loud. She soon came to regret that she had ever learnt how to understand the printed word.

Nancy narrated dreadful crimes that warlocks had committed, so heinous it made her blood run cold just to say the words; of slaughters that had been committed by the lonely wayside; of bodies flung carelessly in deep pits and wells for base demons to feast on. She read too of warlocks who, lying in their beds at dead of night, had conjured such waves of hate that a whole city had turned on itself and by morning had drowned in bloodshed.

The idea of beings that needed only to think of

evil to make wife turn against husband, child against parent, made Nancy's flesh creep and her limbs quail. The terrible descriptions were so real and vivid that the sallow pages seemed to turn red with gore, and the words upon them sounded in her ears as if they were whispered in hollow murmurs by the spirits of the dead.

'And so that is what I am,' Oliver said softly. 'The Tablet of Horus did not lie to me.'

'No wait, Oliver,' Nancy said. 'Look here. This passage talks of another warlock called Edwin Leeford.'

'What of him?' The name seemed familiar, but Oliver couldn't think why.

'It says that he was the worst of warlocks. His power was unmatched and his heart a shrivelled dead thing in his chest.' Nancy's eyes widened. 'But he changed his ways, Oliver. He began to use his magic for good. The book even says that he was rumoured to be helping the Knights of Nostradamus when he was killed in Italy.'

The boy threw the book from him. 'Shut your mouth. I don't want to hear it.' He jumped to his feet, knocking over the chair. 'One good warlock does not change what I am.'

'Oliver,' Nancy said gently, righting the chair. 'You should not be so quick to believe what the Tablet of Horus showed you. I can't say any more than that, but trust me.'

Oliver snorted. 'I trusted you once before. I won't be making that mistake again.' He ran a hand through his lank hair. 'I must see how Sikes and Fagin are getting on.' He stalked out of the room, leaving Nancy alone.

The girl drew her shawl close round her and shivered with inner cold. Warlocks were the cruellest of creatures and, with her help, Fagin was well on his way to turning Oliver into a fully-fledged one.

'I'm sorry,' she whispered into the empty room. 'Oliver, I'm so sorry.'

Chapter XIX

The Break-in

There, there, Bill,' said Fagin as they sat in his den. 'I know it is frustrating, but caution is a virtue.'

'But it has been a whole week,' Sikes growled. 'It is time that we make our move on Brownlow's house.'

'Not at all,' replied Fagin firmly.

'If you won't help me, I'll do it myself.' Sikes leant back in his chair and crossed his arms.

'It hasn't been properly gone about.' Fagin was turning pale with anger. 'Don't tell me how to do this job!'

'But I will tell you,' retorted Sikes. 'Who are you that's not to be told? I tell you that Toby Crackit has been hanging about Brownlow's place for a week and he thinks that he has found one soft spot.'

'So why didn't you say that to begin with, Bill?' said Fagin, cooling off as the other grew heated. 'Of course we must act.' He held out a hand to be shaken.

Sikes thrust aside Fagin's hand, with some disdain. 'Let it come off as soon as you like. Tonight, I reckon. Crackit was over the garden wall the night afore last, sounding the panels of the door and shutters. The house has protective charms all over it, but he's sure he can get in.'

'As you like, Bill, as you like,' replied Fagin. 'I presume you won't need any more to help except Oliver?'

Sikes nodded. 'How is the boy?'

'Oliver is –' Fagin stopped and looked over at Nancy who was by the fire. The old man's forehead became scoured with even more frown lines.

'Why, you don't mind the old girl, do you, Fagin?' Sikes asked at length. 'You've known her long enough to trust her, or the Devil's a fairy-tale princess in a ballgown. She ain't one to cause trouble. Are you, Nance?'

'I should think not!' replied the young lady, drawing her chair up to the table and putting her elbows upon it.

'No, no, my dear, I know you're not,' said Fagin, 'but –' and again the old man paused.

'But what?' enquired Sikes.

'I didn't know whether she mightn't p'r'aps be out

of sorts, you know, as she was the other night,' replied Fagin. 'She did try and put a curse on us and she seems awful fond of the boy.'

At this confession, Nancy burst into a loud laugh and shook her head with an air of defiance. 'I was upset before. Bill had hurt me arm and it wasn't right you hittin' Oliver like that.' Nancy shrugged. 'But he seems happy with his lot and so am I.'

Nancy's words seemed to have the effect of reassuring both gentlemen, for Fagin nodded his head with a satisfied air as did Sikes.

'Now, Fagin,' said Nancy with a laugh, 'tell Bill at once, about Oliver!'

'Aye, I will, my dear,' said Fagin, patting her on the cheek. 'It is most uncommon,' he offered. 'Oliver has taken to the dark like a sea serpent to water!'

'That's good, isn't it?' demanded Sikes.

'It is, it is. There's no doubt he's the boy for you, Bill.' Fagin laid his finger on the side of his nose and grinned frightfully.

'Are you sure he can be trusted?' Sikes asked. 'I don't want him turning on us once we're in Brownlow's house.'

'Have him, Bill!' said Nancy. 'I would, if I was in your place. I've spent time with him, reading that book about warlocks and taking down the names of the weapons.

He's turned evil, proper.' A flicker of sadness passed across Nancy's face. 'Depend upon it, he's a safe one, Bill.'

'I know he is,' rejoined Fagin. 'He's been in good training this last week, and it's time he began to do some work for us before the Brotherhood take him back.' He shrugged. 'If he gives you any lip, frighten him a bit and he will come back into line.'

'Frighten him!' echoed Sikes. 'It'll be no sham frightening, mind you. If he betrays me in any way once we get into the work, you won't see him alive again.'

'Think about what you're saying, Bill,' Fagin cautioned. 'The Brotherhood won't be best pleased if you hurt him.'

'I don't care about the Brotherhood, and why should I? They expelled my forefather, Sköll, from their pack,' said Sikes. 'Mark my words. If Oliver crosses me, he will die.'

The old man frowned. 'I'm not happy, Bill. We really don't want to make an enemy of the Brotherhood.'

Sikes shrugged. 'The plan is set then. We go tonight, when Brownlow and his servants lie in bed.'

'Be sure to get me a handkerchief with Brownlow's initials,' Fagin said.

'If I get in the house, I could just pull his head off for you,' Sikes replied. 'Why even bother with his soul? Let's just kill him.'

'No,' Fagin snapped. 'I want his soul. That man and his Knights are responsible for killing most of my kind. I want to toy with him. I want to drive away his friends, the people he loves. I want him to do things so despicable that he will not be able to look at himself in the mirror. I want him driven quite mad with despair and then and only then will I feed on his soul!'

Sikes grinned wolfishly. 'So be it.'

It was the middle of the night when Oliver was awoken. A sharp rain was beating against the windowpanes and a low wind howled.

'Now then!' growled Sikes, as Oliver started up. 'Look sharp, we're leaving. I'm going to collect Crackit from the inn.'

Oliver dressed swiftly and walked into Fagin's parlour. His dreams had been filled with the cries of the children in the burning workhouse, but the sound was no longer soothing. His head ached with it.

Nancy was awake and, scarcely looking at the boy, threw him a large rough cape to button over his shoulders.

'What is this?' Oliver picked at the thick fabric. 'Come now, I can't believe you really care about my warmth.'

Nancy's eyes flashed. 'Take it or leave it.'

'No need to have hurt feelings, Nance,' Dodge said,

coming into the room. 'I don't think warlocks are meant to be polite.' He shook his head. 'You know your problem, Nance? You're far too nice to people who don't deserve it.'

Nancy held the bridge of her nose. 'I hope you're not going to start complaining about Bill. He's the man I love.'

Dodge raised an eyebrow. 'I'm not saying a word. You've known me long enough to guess my thoughts.'

'You're a child, Dodge. You don't understand love.'

'My grandmother loved me.' Dodge's face was suddenly fierce. 'And I know she would never have hurt me, not like the way Sikes hurts you.'

'Enough,' Oliver snapped. 'I really couldn't be any less interested in your little domestic tiff.' He curled his lip. 'Dodge, what are you doing up anyway?'

The other boy shrugged. 'Couldn't sleep.'

Nancy's face became sympathetic. 'Night Market in town?'

Dodge scowled. 'Perhaps.'

'Night Market?' Oliver scoffed. 'Why would that keep you up?'

'Do not worry about my issues, Oliver.' Dodge's voice was terse. 'Focus on your own. I wish you good luck, mate.'

Fagin shuffled into the room. 'Oliver does not need

luck – he needs stealth and cunning.' The soul-stealer hugged himself. 'And he needs to come back with those weapons and Brownlow's initials on a wipe.'

'You'll get what you need, Fagin,' Oliver murmured. 'But you will take this key off me when I return.'

'A promise is a promise,' Fagin said. 'Now tell me, what will you do if you see Brownlow?'

'I will plead my innocence,' Oliver replied coolly. 'I'll tell him that I was breaking into his house against my will and then lead him to a corner and let Sikes rip off his head.'

Dodge gave a low whistle at Oliver's words and Nancy's face paled.

Fagin clapped his hands in delight. 'What a fine plan, my boy, and I do like initiative. But try not to kill Brownlow unless absolutely necessary. I would so like to have my fun with him.'

Oliver shrugged. 'Then let's hope he does not cross my path.'

Sikes put his head round the door. 'I've got Crackit with me. Let's go.'

Bullseye got to his feet and began to pad towards the door, but Sikes shook his head. 'You ain't coming,' he said, looking disdainfully at the wolf.

Bullseye let out a whine of protest.

'I've got Crackit with me, don't need your help.' The

man's face twisted into a sneer. 'Besides, you'd just mess things up anyway. It's all you're good for.'

Bullseye slumped on to his stomach and put his head on his paws, refusing to look at Sikes.

Nancy knelt down and stroked Bullseye's head. 'It's a good thing he doesn't understand you, Bill. You can be awful mean.'

'He understands well enough. He understood me even when he was a pup,' Sikes snapped back. 'Come on, let's go, Oliver.'

Oliver left Fagin, Dodge, Bullseye and Nancy sitting by the fire and followed Sikes down the stairs.

They met Toby Crackit at the bottom. He was a rather small man, with a hunched back. He wore a voluminous black velveteen coat that seemed to swamp him in its folds and thick leather gloves encased his hands.

'This the boy then?' Crackit asked Sikes.

'The name's Oliver.'

The boy had spoken the words softly, but Crackit felt a chill creep across him for Oliver's voice sounded as hollow as an empty coffin. Crackit nodded his head. 'Nice to meet you, Oliver. It's good weather for a break-in.'

When they got into the street, the wind was blowing fiercely and it was raining hard. Gutters overflowed and large pools of water had collected in the road. Oliver caught a glimpse of himself in a puddle that shifted with the wind. A boy with lank hair and red eyes – a boy dead inside.

The moon was large in the sky and gave a faint glimmer, but it aggravated rather than relieved the gloom of the scene, the sombre light only serving to pale that which the street lamps afforded, without shedding any warmer or brighter tints upon the wet house tops and dreary streets. There appeared to be nobody stirring in that quarter of the town. The windows of the houses were all closely shut, and the streets through which they passed were noiseless and empty.

By the time they had turned into the Angel at Islington, a few country waggons were slowly toiling by and now and then a stagecoach, covered with mud, rattled briskly by. Turning down a street, they came across a square, from which place arose a tumult of discordant sounds which filled Oliver Twisted's heart with a strange feeling of dread. Flaming torches flanked the square, spluttering and hissing in the driving rain. The ground was covered nearly ankle-deep with filth and mire; a thick steam perpetually rose from the reeking bodies of the children with nutmeg skin who were kept in cages. The steam mingled with the fog, which hung heavily upon the chimney tops. All the pens in the centre of the large area, and as many temporary pens as could be crowded into the vacant space, were filled with men and women who had the look of Dodge.

'What is this place?' Oliver asked.

''Tis the Night Market,' Crackit said. He nodded at a family who stood in one of the cages, their hands bloody and mangled from lashing out at the bars. 'All here were taken from lands across the sea.' Crackit sniffed. 'I really don't know what all the fuss is about, but their abilities are in much demand and the little ones get shipped off to vampyre families that can afford it.'

Oliver watched as countrymen, city men, vampyres, demons, traders and buyers mingled together in a mass. The cries of the auctioneers, the shouts, oaths and quarrelling on all sides, the ringing of bells and roar of voices, the whooping and yelling resounded from every corner of the market. Vampyres pointed at cages and wrote down their choices on grubby pieces of paper.

The crowding, pushing, driving, beating of the market pressed down on Oliver and the pitiful cry of children that issued from many of the cages took Oliver's mind back to the bloodfarm and the innocents that were held captive there as well. He was surprised to feel the track of a tear on his cheek and he quickly wiped it away, disgusted at his moment of weakness.

Sikes grabbed Oliver's shoulder and elbowed his way through the thickest part of the crowd, bestowing very little attention on the numerous sights and sounds. 'We need to slap through the market,' he whispered. 'We can't stop for idle chat.' He nodded, twice or thrice, to a passing friend and pressed steadily onward, until they were clear of the turmoil, and had made their way through to Pentonville.

The rain gave way to thick fog, which was much heavier than it had been in the early part of the night, and the atmosphere was so damp that, although no rain fell, Oliver's hair and eyebrows had become stiff with the half-frozen moisture.

'Now, young 'un!' said Sikes, looking up at the clock of a nearby church. ''Tis hard upon three. The household will be fast asleep. Are you ready?'

'Ready has nothing to do with it,' Oliver said. 'There is a job to be done, that is all.'

Sikes laughed. 'So eager to steal from your former benefactor. I'm impressed.'

A damp mist rolled towards Oliver as they approached Brownlow's house and spread itself over the dreary rooftops. They still kept walking on, in mud and darkness, through gloomy lanes, until they came within sight of the lights of the house.

'We go round the back,' Crackit said. 'That is where the sweet spot is.'

They walked behind the detached house and surveyed

the wall that bordered it. Crackit took off his gloves and there was a slurping sound as two large, muscular tentacles pushed out of the sleeves of his large coat and flailed in the air.

Crackit's hunched back had disappeared and Oliver realised that the mound under the coat must have been where the tentacles had been hidden, all bunched up and out of sight.

Oliver cocked his head to one side and stared at Crackit. 'Now what exactly are you?'

'My mother was a swamp goblin,' Crackit replied, as he watched small suckers bloom across his tentacles. 'Comes in useful sometimes.' Not pausing to take breath, he climbed the wall in a twinkling.

'The boy next,' said Crackit from the other side. 'Hoist him up. I'll catch hold of him.'

Before Oliver had time to look round, Sikes had caught him under the arms and, in three or four seconds, he and Crackit were lying on the grass on the other side. Sikes followed directly, springing over the wall in one bound.

They stole cautiously towards the house. Not a word was spoken as they stepped through the marshy ground of the garden.

For a moment, Oliver thought he saw strange objects in the gaunt trees, whose branches waved grimly to and fro, but realised it was just leaves stirring gently in the night wind. There was a dull sound of falling water not far off; like a quiet musical accompaniment for the agents of death and destruction that were at Brownlow's door. Oliver had never seen Brownlow's house from the back. It looked ruinous and decayed in the moonlight.

Crackit, with Oliver and Sikes in tow, softly approached the porch. He pointed to a low window and raised the latch of the shutter to reveal a little lattice window, about five feet and a half above the ground. He placed his hand against the glass, the suckers attaching themselves, and the window gave a low fizz as sparks flew off it. Crackit grinned as it swung open. 'All done.'

The aperture was so small that Oliver could see how Brownlow had overlooked keeping the charm on it strong.

'Now listen,' whispered Sikes, drawing a dim lantern from his pocket, and throwing the glare full on Oliver's face. 'You're going to get through there. Take this light, go to the street door, unfasten it and let us in.'

Oliver nodded.

Crackit produced his lantern and, placing it on the ground, he planted himself firmly beneath the window and made a knot of his two tentacles. This was no sooner done than Crackit instructed Oliver to step on the looped tentacles and, with a mighty heave, he swung the boy upwards.

Oliver soared through the air. He held on to the lantern with one hand, but with the other, he grabbed the window ledge and pulled himself up and through the opening. He moved swiftly through the house. Memories of his time here made something inside him ache and a small voice from deep within told him that what he was about to do was wrong. He ignored it and, reaching the front door, he unbolted it and let Crackit and Sikes into the house.

'Good work,' Sikes said. 'Now take us to the Knights' Armoury.'

Oliver led them up a flight of stairs, but Sikes stopped them on the first landing. 'Wait,' he said in a low whisper. 'I hear something.'

There was a soft creak, like a foot on the stairs, and then a voice. 'Brownlow, is that you?' Mrs Bedwin called. 'You are home late.' She appeared at the top of the stairs, a frail figure in a white nightgown and a frilly cap on her head.

Her eyes widened with pleasure as she saw Oliver. 'You came back –' she began, but stopped as she saw Sikes and Crackit. 'Are you all right, Oliver?' Her voice was sharp. 'What are you doing with these men?'

Oliver had not been worried about any encounters.

He thought he would lie or injure, whatever was easier to gain access to the Knights' Armoury, but now he found he could do neither. 'I am here of my own free will.' The words escaped from Oliver's mouth. 'You should go before you get hurt.'

'I don't believe you,' Mrs Bedwin said. 'You are being controlled. You just don't know it.'

'Get out of our way, old woman.' Sikes stalked towards her, climbing the stairs one at a time.

Mrs Bedwin opened her mouth and screamed. Her voice was louder than thunder, shriller than the screech of a steam train.

'She's a bloody banshee!' Crackit cried. He covered his ears and dropped to the ground.

'I'll rip her throat out.' Sikes dropped to his knees and began to transform. He threw his head back and howled even as the seam of his jacket tore and his fingers lengthened and then curled into claws. Still Mrs Bedwin screamed. Her eyes were filled with fear, but she did not move from her position on the stairs.

Sikes was now fully changed and his muzzle opened to show a jaw filled with razor-sharp teeth. Bunching up his muscles, he got ready to leap at Mrs Bedwin.

'No!' Oliver cried and, in that moment, he found a sliver of goodness in himself again. The nightmare that the Tablet of Horus had shown began to shatter. 'Leave her alone!' He threw himself in front of Sikes, but the wolfman grabbed his collar and hurled him to one side as easily as if he was a small piece of kindling.

Adjusting his massive shoulders, Sikes wheeled himself about once again, ready to spring up the stairs and attack the banshee. Mrs Bedwin's scream became even more piercing, a spike in the brain, and so powerful that Oliver could see the waves of it on the air, pushing Sikes back.

A trail of stickiness flowed from the old wound on his head, but Oliver could see that he was not suffering as much as Mrs Bedwin. Sweat was beading on her brow and her face was haggard. The old woman would not be able to keep up her defence for much longer.

For the first time since Dodge had given him the key, Oliver felt a spark of the Rage. He clung on to it and willed the spark to turn into a blaze.

Mrs Bedwin's scream continued to tear at his ears, but it was not the worst pain. As Oliver fought the key's control and tried to harness his power, his whole head felt like it was caught in a vice. He could almost feel his skull collapsing under the pressure. But he did not stop. The key became hot on his chest and the more he concentrated on the Rage, the hotter the key became.

Sikes was still battling against the banshee's call and

had managed to climb two steps as Mrs Bedwin's scream began to rasp and croak.

Oliver felt the Rage finally catch alight and he realised how much he had missed its heat. It filled him. Swiftly, he put a hand in the air and drew a symbol, a perfectly round circle. His fingers continued to move of their own accord as if they had always known how to do this. Then a red orb appeared and surrounded Mrs Bedwin just as her voice finally faltered and she dropped to her knees with exhaustion.

With a snarl, Sikes struck at the orb and Oliver felt something inside him crack in response. Sikes struck out again at the orb and Oliver could feel his reserve of power splinter apart. Gritting his teeth, he held on to the last shards of his magic and kept the orb intact. The top of his lip felt wet and Oliver realised that his nose was running with blood. The vice around his head tightened even more and the edges of his vision began to turn black.

'Sikes, leave her. We've got to go,' Crackit called, scrambling down the stairs. 'I can hear a coach. Brownlow must be back.' He looked around him wildly before plunging deeper into the house, searching for a way out.

A carriage door slammed shut outside and Brownlow strode through the door. The old man froze as he spied

Sikes on the stairs, and then his pistol was drawn and he was racing up them.

Sikes turned from Mrs Bedwin and leapt for Brownlow instead. They met in a tangle of teeth, metal and fury.

Oliver could feel the orb around Mrs Bedwin fading, but he could not prevent it. The stairs swam before his eyes as he tried to stand.

There was a flash. A loud noise, smoke, a cry and then a crash. Oliver staggered back, his vision fading quickly. He felt like his head was made of glass and it had broken.

Sikes appeared before him, a ragged wound in his side. The wolf had begun to fade, but Sikes still had strength and grabbed Oliver by the collar and dragged the boy up.

'Run, before more of the Knights come,' Sikes said. 'Brownlow is down.'

'I can't,' Oliver said. 'My head, I don't feel right.'

Sikes's hands tightened on Oliver's collar and for a moment he thought how easy it would be to break the troublesome boy's neck. 'I ain't leaving you,' he said instead. 'You're worth too much. Clasp your arm round my neck.' Oliver did as he was told and Sikes carried him forward and down the stairs.

Oliver felt his heart clench as he looked at the

still figure of Brownlow, who lay on a higher step. Brownlow had been kind to him, wanted to make him an apprentice, and Oliver had repaid him by letting Sikes and Crackit into his house.

'I'm sorry,' Oliver murmured to Brownlow as Sikes walked through the door, wishing that the old man could hear his words.

'Aye, you should be,' growled Sikes. 'Why did you protect that old banshee?'

'Because it was the right thing to do,' Oliver whispered, and his eyes fluttered shut.

Chapter XX

Where Nancy and Dodge make a rather Important Decision

'Brownlow fired and hit Sikes,' Crackit told Fagin, his sharp face weary. 'I'd already cut and was over the garden wall, but waited when I heard Sikes coming. We scudded like the wind and went through hedge and ditch to come back here.' He shook his head at the memory. 'How's Bill?'

'In a lot of pain,' Fagin said absently. 'He was hit with a silver bullet and it went deep. Nancy is trying to get it out.'

'And how about the boy?'

'He sleeps,' Fagin muttered. 'And he may never awaken.'

'Well, you can't blame Sikes for the boy's state.' Crackit took a leaf from his hair. 'He carried him on his back the whole time, despite his wounds. We stopped once, to try and get him to walk, but the boy's head hung down and his skin was ice-cold. He was like death.'

'He is in death, on the brink at least.' Fagin scowled. 'Stupid boy, he must have used his magic.' Crackit looked confused and Fagin sighed. 'I put a key round his neck to contain his powers,' he explained. 'But he broke the key's control.'

The old man began to rake his hands through his matted mass of red hair, not seeming to notice that he was tearing out clumps of it with each movement. 'His mind must have been pulled asunder. The pieces may never be put back together.'

Crackit shredded the leaf with one of his tentacles, the pieces falling to the floor like crushed fairy wings. 'The boy's magic was impressive,' he said. 'There was this banshee, a mighty powerful one, but Oliver put an orb around her and she dropped to the ground like a stone and shut up mighty quick as well.'

'Impressive magic indeed.' Fagin looked thoughtful and, finally noticing the red clumps of hair in his hands, let his arms drop to his sides. He sighed. 'The Brotherhood is going to be furious when they hear of his state. It may be time for me to leave London, if this doesn't come good.'

'Oh, this is your mess, Fagin.' Nancy walked into the room, her hands stained with blood. 'You ain't going nowhere.'

'How's Bill?' Crackit asked.

Nancy sniffed. 'I've got the bullet out and Dodge helped keep him pinned down, but Bill is awful sick.'

Crackit put his hat on his head. 'I'm terribly sorry to hear that, Nance. Tell Bill I'm thinking of him,' he said gruffly. 'But I'm not staying around here, especially if the Brotherhood are involved. I ain't survived this long hanging about when trouble like that is brewing.' He dipped his head and left the room, his hastily fleeing footsteps clattering down the steps.

'Crackit is right,' Nancy said fiercely. 'Bill should have never got involved with the likes of you. Look at the state of him now.'

'My dear, do not fret. Bill will heal fast enough.' Fagin waved a bony hand in dismissal. 'The lupine always do. It is Oliver I am worried about. The longer he sleeps the more likely it becomes that he will never wake up. How do you put back together a broken mind?'

'Perhaps it is better that you don't.' Nancy's eyes cast downwards. 'Perhaps it is better if he rots in that bed.'

'What!' cried Fagin in amazement. 'You put a curse on me for hitting the boy and now you want him to rot?'

'Aye, I mean it,' returned the girl, meeting his gaze. 'I shall be glad to have him gone, and to know that the warlock's evil will never be unleashed on the world. I know I'm a bad 'un and Bill is no angel, but that boy could be the end of everything.'

'Exaggeration!' said Fagin scornfully. 'You should be proud of the work we have done with Oliver. We took that young boy and made him bone-deep evil – no element of good rests in his breast.' He smiled, showing sharp teeth. 'No, Oliver is a rare gem.' He rubbed at his crusted lips. 'If only he would wake up, his mind reassembled, then we could give him to the Brotherhood and collect our reward. We need something. None of our other schemes have come good.'

'How did he break his mind anyway?' Nancy asked, interested despite herself.

Fagin swiftly explained about the key. 'According to Crackit, Oliver defeated a banshee and saved both him and Bill,' the old man said. 'Oliver will be a fine warlock, the finest perhaps.'

Nancy felt cold and hugged herself. She thought of the blood that warlocks of the past had shed and of the horror that Oliver could still release. She had spoken her mind, too freely perhaps, but she would not change it. The boy was too dangerous to live and she hoped he would never, ever wake up.

'Nancy,' a weak cry came from the adjacent room. 'Nancy.'

'Bill is awake. I must go to him.'

'Run to him, my girl,' Fagin said, 'and tell him that

I need to speak to him. I must know exactly what happened at Brownlow's house.'

'You'll wait until he's fit,' Nancy snapped back. 'I won't have you tiring him out.'

Fagin inclined his head, but scowled as Nancy flounced from the room.

Sikes was lying on the bed, wrapped in his greatcoat, by way of a dressing gown, and displaying a set of features in no degree improved by the cadaverous hue of illness and the addition of a soiled nightcap. Bullseye sat at the bedside, eyeing his master with something verging on worry, and now pricking his ears and uttering a low growl as some noise in the street, or in the lower part of the house, attracted his attention.

Seated by the window, busily engaged in patching an old waistcoat, was Dodge.

'What time is it?' Sikes's voice was a croak.

'Don't worry about the time,' Nancy said. 'You must rest.'

'Woman, tell me the time.'

'It has just gone seven,' Dodge offered.

'How do you feel, Bill?' Nancy asked.

'As weak as water.' Sikes shifted restlessly. 'I wonder if Brownlow is feeling much better. Shame I left him breathing. Here, lend us a hand and let me get off this thundering bed anyhow.'

Illness had not improved Sikes's temper for, as the girl raised him up and led him to a chair, he muttered various curses on her awkwardness and struck her across the face.

'Leave off, Bill,' Dodge said, jumping to his feet.

'I'm fine, Dodge,' Nancy said. She held her cheek, her eyes welling up as she worked her jaw. 'It stings a bit, that's all.'

'Whining, are you?' said Sikes. 'Come! Don't stand there snivelling. If you can't do anything better than that, sod off altogether. D'ye hear me?'

'I hear you,' replied the girl, turning her face aside. She caught Dodge staring at her, but she refused to meet his gaze. Nancy forced a laugh. 'Bill, you are in a foul mood. What is wrong with you tonight?'

'I was almost killed, remember?' Sikes barked. 'But I shouldn't be surprised that you don't care. You put a curse on me after all.' He glared at her. 'I bet you're pleased it almost came true.'

'Oh, Bill,' Nancy cried. 'I was just upset. I don't have the power to curse nobody.'

'And so why am I suffering then?' Sikes demanded. 'Between you and the boy, I'm surprised I'm not a corpse.'

'But I thought Oliver saved you from the banshee?' Nancy questioned.

221

'Saved me!' Sikes roared. 'The boy was too busy protecting that old crone.

Nancy went very still. 'Oliver used his magic to save the woman?'

'Aye, if I could have got through that orb he put over her, I would have swiped that banshee's head right off her shoulders.' Sikes peered at Nancy. 'Why you so interested?'

'You are not my only patient today,' Nancy said primly. 'The boy is in a deep sleep and I have to care for him as well. 'Tis good to understand what put him there.'

'Mind that you tell me when he is awake, Nance,' Sikes said in a savage voice. 'Before Fagin, before anyone else, understand. Oliver and I have business to settle.'

Sikes's tone sent a shiver through Nancy. 'He might not wake up at all, you know,' she gabbled. 'Fagin says the longer he sleeps the more likely it is that he will die.'

'Oliver is a fighter,' said Dodge, moving away from the window sill. Nancy jumped; she had almost forgotten the boy was there. 'He'll come back.'

'What foolery is this?' Sikes growled. 'Gone soft as well, Dodge?' Sikes shook his head in disgust. 'I'd expect it from the girl, but not from you.'

'I'm not soft, but I'm not stupid either,' Dodge shot back. 'Oliver is a fighter, that's the long and short of it.'

He strode out, the door slamming behind him.

Sikes curled his lip at Nancy. 'Go on, follow him out as well. I'm sick of your woman's nonsense. And take Bullseye as well.'

Nancy opened her mouth to reply, but instead grabbed the wolf's collar and stalked out of the room. She'd expected to see Fagin in the parlour, but only Dodge was there. He stood by the fire, his hands in his pockets, quite motionless.

Nancy released the wolf's collar, and Bullseye padded over to the fire and dropped down in front it.

'We need to save Oliver.' Dodge's words were softly said and he did not turn round.

Nancy felt her mouth go dry. *Ignore him*, her thoughts screamed. *'Tis safest and wisest.*

Dodge whirled round to face her. 'Did you hear what I said?'

Nancy played with the sash on her dress, looping the fabric round and round her fingers until it cut into her skin. Soon they looked quite blue. 'How could we help him, even if I wanted to?' she said eventually. 'Fagin said his mind is shattered.'

'So we try and put it back together.' Dodge rubbed the back of his neck. 'Nancy, we owe it to him. We tricked Oliver, trapped him, exposed him to the worst of evils and despite everything, he managed to find that little bit of good inside him and help that old woman. You heard what Sikes said.'

'So what you sayin'?' Nancy scoffed. 'That we need to find our little bit of good as well?'

'Yes.' Dodge held her eyes. 'Why is that so ridiculous? We live under Fagin's and Sikes's rule, but we are not them, Nance.' He frowned. 'My grandmother was a good woman. After we were caught and brought to this kingdom, she spent night and day showing me how to become smoke, and she used all her magic to do it.' Dodge's dark eyes looked haunted. 'Once I'd learnt, she told me to run and I did and I never saw her again.' His voice had become hoarse. 'I should have saved her, just as Oliver saved that old woman. And if my grandmother was here, she'd want me to help Oliver.'

Nancy cupped her jaw. It ached from the blow that Sikes had given her earlier and she tried not to think of all the scars and bruises left from his previous beatings. Friends had urged her to leave Sikes, but she never did. *I've chosen to stay with him, in this life, but Oliver never had a choice*, she thought. Yet, when it mattered, and despite all the horrors he had been shown, he chose to save another's life.

Nancy lifted her chin. 'You got a plan?'

Dodge grinned in delight. 'Well, I don't know if you can really call it a plan, but I thought we could go and see

Brownlow. He might know a way to bring Oliver back.'

Nancy nodded. 'All right, we'll try to get a message to the house tonight. But we can't tell a soul. Fagin and Bill would kill us if they found out.'

Dodge nodded solemnly and the wolf in front of the fire gave a low growl.

Chapter XXI

The time arrives for Nancy to meet Brownlow

A dept as she was in all the arts of cunning and dissimulation, over the next two weeks Nancy could not wholly conceal the effect her decision to seek help for Oliver wrought upon her mind. She remembered that both Fagin and Sikes had confided to her their schemes, which had been hidden from all others, and felt guilty about her imminent betrayal of that trust.

Nancy had decided that she would meet with Brownlow that night, as had been arranged by Dodge, but she would drop no clue which could lead to Sikes's discovery.

According to Dodge, Brownlow was weak but very much alive. They had only spoken through written messages that Dodge had delivered and collected from

Brownlow's over the last few days, as Dodge felt that Brownlow would surely recognise him as the boy who had tried to steal his handkerchief if they were to meet in person.

'That's why you have to meet him, Nance,' Dodge had said earlier that day. 'There's a chance he'll listen to you. I'll be nearby watching just in case.'

Nancy, though riddled with guilt and wretchedness, was resolved. 'I'll do it, Dodge.'

She had grown pale and thin over the last two weeks and today she looked very much like a ghost. At times, she took no heed of what was passing before her, or no part in conversations where once she would have been the loudest. At other times, she laughed without merriment and was noisy, and then a moment afterwards, she sat silent and dejected, brooding with her head upon her hands.

It was Sunday night and the bell of the nearest church struck the hour. Sikes and Fagin were talking, but they paused to listen. The girl looked up from the low seat on which she sat reading a book, and listened too. Eleven.

'An hour this side of midnight,' said Sikes, raising the blind to look out and returning to his seat. 'Dark and heavy it is too. A good night for secrets.'

'Why do you say that?' asked Fagin. 'We have no secrets.'

'You're right for once,' replied Sikes gruffly. 'I'm just out of humour that's all.'

Fagin sighed and shook his head despondently. 'As am I. The boy still hasn't awoken and the Brotherhood have said that they want him back tomorrow. What can I do? I have tried everything.'

'Well, he better awaken before that for your sake,' said Sikes. 'Besides, Oliver and I have things to discuss as well.'

'That's the way to talk, my friend.' Fagin ventured to pat him on the shoulder. 'It does me good to hear you so concerned for my welfare and so fond of the boy.'

'Does you good, does it!' cried Sikes. 'Well, I am pleased for that.'

Fagin laughed, as if he were relieved by even this concession. 'I think you are almost healed, Bill. You're much like yourself tonight. Quite like yourself.'

'I don't feel like myself when you lay that withered old claw on my shoulder, so take it away,' said Sikes, casting off Fagin's hand.

'It makes you nervous, Bill, reminds you of being grabbed by Brownlow, does it?' Fagin was determined not to be offended.

'Reminds me of being nabbed by the Devil,' returned Sikes. 'There never was another man with such a face as yours, unless it was your father. Unless you came straight from Beelzebub without any father at all, which I shouldn't wonder at a bit.'

Fagin offered no reply to this compliment, but pulling Sikes by the sleeve, pointed his finger towards Nancy, who had taken advantage of the foregoing conversation to put on her bonnet, and was now leaving the room.

'Hallo!' cried Sikes. 'Nance. Where you going to at this time of night?'

'Not far.'

'What answer's that?' retorted Sikes. 'Do you hear me?'

'I don't know where,' replied the girl.

'Then I do,' said Sikes, more in the spirit of obstinacy than because he had any real objection to the girl going where she wanted. 'Nowhere. Sit down.'

'I'm not well. I told you that before,' rejoined the girl. 'I want a breath of air.'

'Put your head out of the window,' replied Sikes.

'There's not enough there. I want it in the street.'

'Then you won't have it at all,' replied Sikes. With which assurance he rose, locked the door, took the key out and, pulling her bonnet from her head, flung it up to the top of an old press. 'There,' he said. 'Now stop quietly where you are, will you?'

'It's not such a matter as a bonnet would keep me.' Two high spots of colour rode Nancy's cheeks. 'What do you mean, Bill? Do you know what you're doing?'

'Know what I'm – Oh!' cried Sikes, turning to Fagin. 'She's out of her senses, you know, or she daren't talk to me in that way.'

Fagin looked at Nancy very closely. 'She does seem awful keen to go out and for what reason I cannot imagine.'

Nancy managed to plaster a smile on her face. 'I have a reason, but I didn't want to share it.' She sighed. 'I was going to take Bullseye out. You don't know it, but the wolf will foul himself if I don't take him outside, and Bill, you get awful angry with him.'

Sikes's shoulders dropped. 'You want to take Bullseye out? Why didn't you say so before?' He placed two fingers in his mouth and whistled, and the wolf padded into the room from the kitchen.

'Keep each other safe, won't you?' Sikes said.

As he uttered these words, Nancy snatched up her bonnet and held out her hand for the key. 'We will,' she said.

Nancy bid Sikes and Fagin farewell and walked down the stairs, Bullseye at her heels. When they reached the passage, Dodge appeared with a candle.

'What took you so long?' he asked. 'We have to meet him at midnight.' He cast his eyes downwards. 'And what's Bullseye doing with you?'

Nancy laid her finger on her lips and, drawing close,

said, 'Bill wouldn't let me out, so I said I needed to walk Bullseye.' Worry was etched on hers face and she hugged herself tightly. 'I'm worried he suspects something. Maybe we shouldn't go.'

'We have to,' Dodge insisted. 'If we don't turn up tonight, Brownlow will never trust us to meet again.'

'You're right,' Nancy said. 'Also Fagin says that the Brotherhood are coming for Oliver tomorrow, so we need to do this tonight. Make sure you stay close, but don't let Brownlow see you.'

Dodge grinned. 'I will be like smoke.'

The church clocks chimed three-quarters past eleven as two figures and a wolf emerged on London Bridge. One, which advanced with a swift and rapid step, was that of a woman who looked eagerly about her as though in quest of some expected object; the other was a boy, who slunk along in the deepest shadow he could find, with the wolf staying close beside him. He accommodated his pace to hers, stopping when she stopped, and as she moved again, creeping stealthily on, but never allowing himself to gain upon her footsteps.

Thus they crossed the bridge, from the north to the south shore.

It was a very dark night. The day had been unfavourable, and at that hour and place there were few people stirring. Those that were, hurried quickly past, very possibly without seeing, but certainly without noticing, either the woman or the boy and wolf who kept her in view as they scuttled into hiding by the steps of the bridge.

A mist hung over the river, deepening the red glare of the fires that burnt upon the small craft moored off the different wharfs, and rendering darker and more indistinct the murky buildings on the banks.

The old smoke-stained storehouses on either side rose heavy and dull from the dense mass of roofs and gables, and frowned sternly upon water too black to reflect even their lumbering shapes. The tower of old Saint Saviour's Church and the spire of Saint Magnus, so long the giant warders of the ancient bridge, were clearly visible in the gloom.

The girl had taken a few restless turns to and fro, closely watched meanwhile by her hidden observers, Dodge and Bullseye, when the heavy bell of Saint Paul's tolled for the death of another day. Midnight had come upon the crowded city. The palace, the night-cellar, the jail, the madhouse; the chambers of birth and death, of health and sickness; the rigid face of the corpse and the calm sleep of the child: midnight was upon them all.

The hour had not struck two minutes when a grey-haired gentleman alighted from a hackney carriage within a short distance of the bridge and, having dismissed the vehicle, limped towards it. Brownlow had scarcely set foot upon it when the girl started and immediately made towards him.

'Not here,' said Nancy hurriedly. 'I am afraid to speak to you here. Come away, out of the public road, down the steps yonder!'

As she uttered these words, she pointed to the stairs on the southern bank where Dodge and Bullseye hid.

Dodge had been on the point of emerging from his hiding place and regaining the bridge above, when he heard the sound of footsteps and, directly afterwards, of voices almost close at his ear. He slipped into smoke and Bullseye dropped low on his belly. Dodge listened attentively.

'This is far enough,' said Brownlow. 'I will not go any further. Many people would have distrusted you too much to have come even so far, but you see I am willing to humour you.'

'To humour me!' cried Nancy. 'You're considerate indeed, sir. To humour me!'

'Apologies for my short tone,' said Brownlow more gently. 'For what purpose can you have brought me to this strange place? The letters said that you had information on Oliver.'

'I do,' Nancy said.

'Tell me everything. Mrs Bedwin said Oliver brought that wolfman and his tentacled accomplice into the house, but then he cast a spell of protection around her – it makes no sense.'

'Sir, it is a sorry tale, but I will share it with you.' Nancy swiftly told Brownlow everything that had happened to Oliver since he was taken: how his mind was twisted by Fagin, the truth that Oliver was a warlock and that the Brotherhood wanted him desperately and were planning on fetching him the next day. 'Despite the key, he used his magic to protect Mrs Bedwin,' Nancy finished. 'It tore his mind apart and he has not opened his eyes since.'

Brownlow nodded, his face thoughtful. 'Thank you, your explanation makes many things clear to me. Come, let us go where there is light instead of lingering in this dark and dismal hole.'

'I am afraid to speak to you up there,' Nancy replied. She shuddered. 'I have such a fear and dread upon me tonight that I can hardly stand.'

'A fear of what?' asked Brownlow.

'I scarcely know,' said Nancy. 'I wish I did. Horrible thoughts of death, and shrouds with blood upon them, and a fear that has made me burn as if I was on fire, have been upon me all day. I was reading a book tonight, to while the time away, and the same things came into the print.'

'Imagination,' said the gentleman, soothing her.

'No imagination.' Nancy's voice was hoarse. 'I'll swear I saw "coffin" written in every page of the book in large black letters.'

There was something so convincing in her manner that Dodge's flesh crept as he heard Nancy utter these words, and the blood chilled within him. *Maybe I was wrong to make her come here tonight*, he thought.

'Now listen to me,' said Brownlow. 'I can protect you if you need me to, but you must tell me more of Oliver's condition.'

'There is not much more to say,' Nancy replied. 'He lies in a deep sleep and though Fagin has tried many things, Oliver will not awaken.'

'Fagin,' repeated Brownlow. 'He is the soul-stealer, is he not? The one who enslaved Oliver with the key?'

Nancy nodded.

'That man must be delivered up by you,' said Brownlow. 'He is a menace that needs to be stopped.'

'I will not do it! I will never do it!' Nancy lifted her chin. 'Devil that he is, worse than devil maybe, but I will never do that.'

'How about that werewolf?' said Brownlow, who seemed fully prepared for this answer.

'Never!' returned the girl.

'Tell me why.'

'For one reason,' rejoined the girl firmly. 'For as bad a life as he has led, I have led a bad life too. There are many of us who have kept the same courses together and I'll not turn upon them, who might any of them have turned upon me, but didn't, bad as they are.'

'Then,' said the gentleman, 'how do you expect to help Oliver, if he is under Fagin's control? How can I heal him?'

'Give me the cure,' Nancy said.

Brownlow considered her words. 'I will need to go home and consult my books, but I'm sure the boy's mind can be pieced back together. Then he will have the strength to escape the sleep that claims him.'

'How will you give me the remedy?' Nancy asked.

'Meet me here in the morning,' Brownlow replied. 'I will give you a medicine for Oliver.'

'I will,' said Nancy. 'I have been a liar and among liars from a little child, but I will meet you here at seven, I swear.'

'You are a good person and a true friend to Oliver,' Brownlow murmured. 'I wish you to be the better for it. What can I do to serve you?'

'Nothing,' replied Nancy.

'You will not persist in saying that,' rejoined the gentleman, with a soft voice and emphasis of kindness. 'I had a daughter once, Agnes, and I did not help when I should have. I only judged her because she loved a man, a warlock, and I cast her aside. I will not make that mistake again. Think now. What can I do?'

'Nothing, sir.' Nancy began to weep. 'You can do nothing to help me. I am past all hope, indeed.'

'You put yourself beyond hope,' said the gentleman. 'The past need not be your prisoner.'

'No, sir, I am chained to my old life and to the man I love. I must go home.'

'Home!' repeated Brownlow with a snort.

'Home,' rejoined Nancy. 'To such a home as I have raised for myself. Let us part.'

'Until the morning.' Brownlow ascended the stairs.

'Until the morning.' Nancy watched Brownlow go and then turned to look into the shadows. 'Did you hear all that, Dodge?' she asked after a moment.

Dodge emerged from the darkness. 'I did. Brownlow is really going to help us.'

Nancy nodded wearily. 'Come, I have been gone too long. Bill will be watching for me.'

Bullseye suddenly gave a low growl, bounded up the stairs and tore across the bridge.

'Bullseye!' Dodge hollered, starting out after the wolf. 'Where you going?'

Nancy touched Dodge's arm. 'Let him stretch his legs. Bullseye will find his way home and meet us by the door. He is the cleverest creature I ever did see.'

Dodge nodded, watching the wolf disappear from sight. He turned to Nancy and saw that her face was very pale. 'I heard what you said about feeling the dread upon you. I'm sorry I made you come out tonight.'

'Do not fret, Dodge. I'm so pleased I did this thing tonight – it might be the one good deed of my life. Come, let us go home.'

Chapter XXII

Fatal consequences

It was nearly one o'clock, the dead of night, and the streets were silent and deserted. Even sound appeared to slumber, and dissolution and riot had staggered home to dream. It was at this still and silent hour that Bullseye raced through the streets, his claws clattering against the cobbles.

For his whole life, Bullseye's brother had hated him. It hadn't been Bullseye's fault that he had come to this world blind or that he was born as a wolf, unable to shift into human form. It hadn't been his fault that their mother had plucked an eyeball from Sikes's socket, as he lay defenceless as a babe, and sewn it into Bullseye's head, giving Bill a glass eye in exchange.

Bullseye gave a low whine as he remembered what Sikes had done to their mother the first time he had lost control and turned into the wolf. He still remembered how he had stood and watched as Bill had dug the grave for their mother, a very small hole for the pieces that had remained.

No, his whole life, Bill had treated Bullseye as if he was the bane of his existence. But Bill had kept him close, the two of them being able to understand each other as only true brothers could.

Now Bullseye would be able to repay Bill's nurture with the information of what Nancy and Dodge had done. The wolf felt a niggle of guilt. Nancy had always treated him nicely and Dodge wasn't bad either, but Bullseye knew he couldn't keep such a secret from his brother.

The wolf arrived at Fagin's house and let out a high, pure howl. Bullseye saw the blind in the window twitch and knew that Bill had seen him.

Sikes thundered down the stairs and opened the door. 'Where's Nance?' he asked. 'Why are you alone?'

Bullseye did not reply, but simply slipped past Sikes and hurtled up the stairs and into the parlour where Fagin sat.

'What is this?' said Fagin as Sikes's burly frame came into the room. 'Where are Nancy and Dodge?'

'That is what I intend to find out.' Sikes looked down at the wolf. 'Come now, Bullseye, tell me.'

Fagin laughed. 'I don't see how you plan to understand him, Bill, unless you turn into the wolf yourself.'

Sikes turned his bloodshot gaze on Fagin. 'I will understand Bullseye well enough as I am. He is my brother after all.'

Fagin's eyes widened. 'Well, I –' He stopped. 'Bill, I don't understand. Why have you never said?'

Sikes shrugged. 'Bullseye is my business, my brother and my responsibility. It's got nothing to do with anyone else.' He turned to the wolf. Bullseye's lips were quivering so violently, and his face was so altered by the emotions which went through him, that Sikes involuntarily drew back in his chair and surveyed him with a look of real affright. 'What now?' cried Sikes. 'What do you look at your brother so for?'

Bullseye opened his mouth, but the passion in his chest was so great that the power of speech was for the moment gone.

'Damn!' said Sikes, almost to himself. 'He's gone mad.'

'No, no,' explained Bullseye with a whine, 'I'm not mad. What I've got to tell you, Bill, will make you feel worse than me.'

'Aye?' returned Sikes with an incredulous air. 'Tell away! Look sharp! Nance will be home soon and I don't want her to see me talking to a mangy cur like you.'

Bullseye growled at the insult and bared his teeth.

'Speak, will you!' Sikes said. 'Or if you don't, it shall be for want of breath. Open your mouth and say what you've got to say. Out with it!'

'Suppose that lad that's laying in the bed, in the bedroom yonder, had touched Nancy's heart,' Bullseye began.

Sikes turned round to stare at the room where Oliver was sleeping. 'Well!' he said, resuming his former position. 'I would not be that surprised. Nancy can have a foolishly soft heart.'

'Suppose that lad's illness,' pursued Bullseye, 'made Nancy and Dodge seek out Brownlow for a cure, and then have a meeting with him in the street to tell him everything that has been done to Oliver?'

'No.' Sikes had gone very white. 'She would not. Dodge would not.'

'Would not what?' Fagin demanded, looking between Bullseye and Sikes. All he had been able to hear was the wolf's yips, barks, whines and howls.

'My brother thinks Nancy and Dodge met with Brownlow this evening to seek a cure for Oliver.'

Fagin's face instantly became distorted, and his eyes became so red and bloodshot that he looked less like a man than some hideous phantom, moist from the grave and worried by an evil spirit. 'Get your brother to tell you again,' he said slowly. 'But repeat his words to me one line at a time for me to hear.'

'I went with her to London Bridge,' Bullseye whined, and Sikes repeated. 'Where she met Brownlow.'

'Did she now?' Fagin said.

'Brownlow asked what had happened to Oliver and she told it all.' Bullseye revealed.

'What, every word without a threat, without a murmur?' cried Fagin, half mad with fury.

'Yes,' replied Bullseye, his one eye sad. 'That's what happened, but Nancy and Dodge just wanted to help the boy.'

'Hell's fire!' cried Sikes. 'Let me go! I will find Dodge and Nancy on the street and tear them apart.' He rushed from the room and darted, wildly and furiously, down the stairs.

'Bill, Bill!' cried Fagin, following him hastily. 'A word. Only a word.'

The word would not have been exchanged if Sikes had been able to open the door. He began smashing at it, meaty palms quickly becoming claws as his transformation began to take place.

'Let me out,' growled Sikes. 'Don't speak to me; it's not safe.'

His teeth were so tightly compressed that the strained jaw seemed to want to start through his skin. 'Let me out, I say!' Bristles were springing out all over Sikes's skin and there was a snap of bone as the bottom bit of his jaw elongated and a muzzle began to thrust from his face.

'Hear me speak a word,' rejoined Fagin. 'Do not go into the street and do your violence there. Stay here, where secrets will be kept – wait for Nancy and Dodge to come back here and have your revenge. I will wake the boys and take them with me so that you will have peace.'

Bullseye was now at the top of the stairs. 'Don't listen to him, brother. Don't hurt Nancy,' he pleaded. 'She just wanted to help Oliver; she did not really betray you.'

Sikes made no reply, but dropped to all fours and padded back up the stairs. He lay in front of the fire and seethed and waited.

Fagin scuttled like a beetle into the back rooms. He roused Charley and the rest of the boys. ''Tis time to go, my boys,' he whispered. 'Time for a new start. Pack light.'

'What about, Dodge?' Charley asked.

Fagin shrugged, his shoulders right up to his ears. 'I fear things will not end well for him, Charley, or Nance for that matter. Better to leave Dodge behind.'

And for once Charley Bates could find nothing to laugh about.

*

The house was completely empty except for Sikes and Bullseye when Dodge and Nancy came through the door. Sikes had listened as Fagin had led all the boys out of the house. He knew they weren't coming back and he did not care.

Nancy stopped as she saw the wolfman by the fire. 'Why, Bill, who's upset you?' she asked with a hurried and startled look.

'Come closer!' said the wolfman.

'Of course, my love.' Nancy took a step forward, but Dodge held on to her arm.

'Be careful, Nance,' he said.

'It is just Bill!' said Nancy with a confident expression. 'Fagin has probably upset him and got the wolf up, and look, Bullseye is safe at home again.' She shook her head. 'Naughty to run off like that, Bullseye.'

The wolf gave a low whine in response.

'Come closer, Nance,' Sikes ordered in his guttural wolf voice. 'I feel like I have not seen you properly in a long time.'

'Why, here I am,' Nancy said. 'No need to miss me.'

'Miss you?' said Sikes, padding towards her. 'Miss you? Miss you a liar, miss you a betrayer, miss you a dead woman walking.'

'Bill,' said Nancy, in a low voice of alarm. 'Why are you saying such horrible things?'

Sikes reared up on his hind legs, seven foot of muscles, teeth and fur slavering in front of her. 'You know, you she-devil!' returned the wolfman. 'You were watched tonight; every word you said was heard.'

Dodge jumped in front of Nancy. 'It was my fault. I made her do it.'

Sikes stood regarding Dodge for a few seconds, with dilated nostrils and heaving breast; and then, grasping him by the head and throat, dragged him into the middle of the room. Dodge instantly tried to change into smoke, but Sikes was quicker and swung the boy towards the fireplace. Dodge's head connected with a crack on the stone mantelpiece and lolled lazily to one side, blood raining down from a deep gash in his forehead and running over his closed eyes. With a growl, Sikes threw Dodge to the floor.

'Bill, Bill!' gasped Nancy, running to Dodge's still body. 'What have you done?'

'Not enough,' Sikes said. 'Not enough by half.' He hauled her up by her arms.

'Spare my life, Bill,' sobbed Nancy, clinging to him. 'Bill, dear Bill, you cannot have the heart to kill me. Oh, think of all I have given up, of what we have shared. I will not loosen my hold, you cannot throw me off.' She strove to lay her head upon his breast. 'For your own sake, for mine, stop before you spill more blood!'

'Get off me!' Sikes howled. 'I will not let you charm me with your honeyed words.' The wolfman struggled violently to release his arms and, as they burst free, one of his claws sliced against her throat.

He felt something inside himself die as he looked at Nancy's upturned face that almost touched his own. As he saw all colour drain from it, as he felt the blood soak his skin and watched her eyes close.

It was a ghastly sight to look upon. The murderer staggered backward to the wall and, shutting out the sight with his hand, let out a long, mournful howl. Bullseye crept towards Nancy and pushed his muzzle in her warm, black hair, and a single tear left his bloodshot eye.

The night continued to swallow Sikes's howls, but eventually they stopped and he called Bullseye to his side.

'We leave this place, brother,' he murmured.

'Where will we go?' Bullseye asked.

'I do not know, but we will destroy Oliver first,' Sikes said. 'This I vow. It is his fault that Nancy is dead and he must be made to pay.'

'The Knights may pursue us once they hear of what has happened to Nancy. Brownlow knows her now,' Bullseye said. 'We shouldn't kill Oliver. No, that would be foolish. Let us take him with us as our hostage. Perhaps we can find the Brotherhood and hand him over.'

Sikes bared his teeth, but eventually nodded and lumbered towards Oliver's room. He looked down at the sleeping boy. Oliver's lips were blue and his skin had a sickly pallor to it, but he still breathed.

'We take him now,' Sikes said to his brother, throwing Oliver over his shoulder. 'And once we escape the city good and proper, I will kill him.'

Chapter XXIII

Where Oliver meets someone from his

past and a woodcutter calls

Still Oliver slept, even as Nancy's body grew cold and Dodge lay unmoving. In his dream, Oliver was on a desolate hilltop. It felt like he had been there a long time, but he couldn't know for sure for the sun neither seemed to rise nor fall in this place. A violent wind whipped round him, cold fingers raking at his skin through thin clothes.

Grey cloud hung in the air in front of him. Despite this, Oliver could clearly see a steep valley laid out before him, but he had no interest in venturing there. He wanted to stay exactly where he was.

'What are you doing here?' a voice said behind him.

Oliver whipped round to see a woman with a blue bonnet tied neatly under her chin. She looked familiar.

'Do I know you?' Oliver asked.

'You don't remember meeting me before?' the woman questioned.

Oliver shook his head.

'It does not matter.' The woman's voice was soft. 'You are in Otherwhere. This place is not for you, 'tis only for the dead and you are not.'

'I would be better off if I was,' Oliver murmured.

The woman tutted. 'You don't know what you are saying. You have to leave here. It is not safe for you.'

'And the world is not safe with me in it,' Oliver replied. 'This is the best place for me.'

The lady looked over her shoulder. 'He'll be here soon. Wake yourself up, Oliver, and leave.'

Oliver shook his head. 'I will not.'

The woman began to pace backwards and forwards, trampling the grass beneath her feet. She stopped as a distant whistle reached her ears.

'That is him, that's his whistle.' The woman's voice trembled. 'We have to go.'

'Who is he?' Oliver asked.

'There is no time.' The woman's eyes scanned the valley, planning her route.

'Tell me or I won't run,' Oliver insisted.

'The woodcutter.' She almost spat the words. 'Man and axe, axe and man. Those that are not quick enough or smart become timber for him. His house is made of our bones and we burn in the fire in his grate, burn as kindlewood.'

Oliver shuddered. He had thought himself beyond fear, beyond caring, but as the whistle filled his ears, he felt his palms prickle with sweat.

'I have magic . . .' he began.

'You do?' The woman sounded inordinately pleased, proud even. She shook her head. 'I'm afraid magic has no sway in this place.'

She started down the hill, her shoes gliding across the grass. Oliver was right beside her, the woodcutter's whistle at their backs. Oliver could almost feel it clawing his neck. 'Where will we go?' he asked.

'We'll go across the bog, and if we make it to the stones, we'll be safe,' she said. 'The woodcutter will not be able to cross the threshold.'

'And if we don't?'

'Then that is the end, for both of us.' The woman's voice began to crack. 'The woodcutter cannot be negotiated with. He cannot be defeated. He is as old as the hills and as strong as thunder.' She looked over her shoulder again as the whistling reached a deafening pitch and her hand fluttered to her mouth to hold in a scream.

Oliver followed her gaze to see a man standing on the hilltop looking down at them. He was dressed in trousers, ragged and black, and wore a necklet made of bones and teeth. The woodcutter's hair was long and white and stained with red at the tips, and his arms up to his elbows were covered in blood and gore. From his hand he swung an axe that was so big it touched the ground.

The man stopped whistling and brought the axe to his face, stroking it across his cheek, running his tongue along the blade.

The woman pulled at Oliver's sleeve, but he could not tear his eyes from the axeman.

The woodcutter's shoulders began to shake and a laugh echoed across the hills, manic and screeching. He held out his axe like a gift and pointed it at Oliver.

'You cannot have him,' the woman whispered, coming to stand in front of Oliver. 'You cannot have him.' She repeated the words again and again until they became a scream.

The woodcutter stopped laughing, leaving only the echo of the woman's yelled words. He slung the axe over his shoulder and charged towards them.

Oliver was no longer frozen. He grabbed the woman's arm and they ran from the woodcutter and down, down into the valley. He could smell the bog before he saw it, a hollow in the slope of the valley filled with foul-smelling peat and silt.

The woman waded into the bog, the crinoline beneath

her dress instantly becoming sodden. Oliver splashed in after her. The bog welcomed his body eagerly, the mud clinging to him in a cold wet embrace. Oliver could feel it weighing down his legs, filling his shoes.

The woman was struggling as well and the whistle was all around them.

'He will not take you,' the woman said. 'No, he will not.' She hurried forward, but her foot connected on a small hillock of grass and she went sprawling into the mud, her cloak spreading out around her like an ink blot.

Oliver gripped her arms and pulled her up. She gave a gasp of pain.

'Go,' she said, 'my ankle is twisted. He cannot get you. Go straight and get into the stones.' She pointed at a ring of boulders that was about a hundred paces ahead.

'Who are you?' Oliver asked. 'Why would you sacrifice yourself for me?'

'If I tell you, do you promise to go?' Her words were almost drowned out by the woodcutter's whistling that echoed across the bog, but he still couldn't be seen.

Oliver nodded.

The woman reached under her bonnet and unlaced it. 'Look upon me,' she said, taking off the bonnet. 'Don't you see who I am?'

Oliver stared at the woman. Her face was badly pitted by scars and her blonde hair grew only in clumps on her head, but he could see that she had once been beautiful. Emerald eyes stared out at him, eyes that were as familiar as his own, and he could see himself in the curve of her cheek.

The woman smiled. 'I am your mother, Oliver, and I need you to listen to me. The woodcutter is at the bottom of this hill and he is coming. You must run.'

'No, I can't leave you.'

'You promised.'

'I didn't know you were my mother,' Oliver shot back.

'Oliver, I have stayed in this cursed place because I could not pass until I knew you were safe, until you had become the person I knew you could be. The world's saviour.'

Oliver laughed despite himself. His whole life he had dreamed of knowing his mother, and now he did, all he would be is a disappointment. 'I wish I could lie to you, but I am no one's saviour. I'm evil.'

His mother placed a hand on his shoulder. 'You are not evil. You are my son.'

Oliver felt the warmth of her certainty go through him, but he fought it. 'I am evil,' he gasped out. 'I took Sikes and Crackit to the armoury.' His voice began to shake. 'Mrs Bedwin was on the stairs and she would not let us pass. She began to scream and scream.'

'Bless her heart,' Oliver's mother murmured. 'She's

old, but one of the fiercest banshees to have trodden the earth.'

'You know Mrs Bedwin?' Oliver asked in amazement. His mother nodded. 'What happened next?'

Oliver wrapped his arms about himself. 'Sikes was going to attack her and so I used a protective charm. I used my magic.'

'So you saved her,' his mother pointed out. 'Oliver, you were wrong to take Sikes and Crackit to the house, but you made it right. You saved Mrs Bedwin.'

'But what of Brownlow? He fought Sikes and he wasn't moving at the end. That's my fault.'

His mother looked sad. 'Sikes hurt Brownlow, not you, and I do not think that Brownlow is dead. I'd feel it, I'm sure.' Her eyes became shiny with tears. 'But if I'm wrong and he is dead, then it is even more important that you accept your destiny. You must become humanity's protector, a leader for the Knights.' She touched his face. 'I will not lie to you, dear heart. You have darkness in you. You are a warlock just like your father, my darling Edwin, but that is what will make you extraordinary, just as he was. Your father used his dark for good.'

Oliver's breath became a gasp as he suddenly remembered Nancy reading to him in Fagin's den. She had spoken of Edwin Leeford, of a warlock who had become good. Oliver's mind wheeled back even further and he was back with Grimwig and Brownlow in the study. The two Knights were arguing. Brownlow was upset because Grimwig had mentioned his daughter, Agnes Brownlow, and the man she loved, Edwin Leeford.

The whistling pulled Oliver from his tangle of thoughts. The sound was all around them now and Oliver looked up to see that the woodcutter was just twenty paces away, stalking through the water.

'Oliver,' his mother said, 'you won't make it to the stones. You have to wake yourself up. Take on your destiny. It is the only way you can escape the woodcutter.'

Oliver wasn't really listening. 'You are Brownlow's daughter, Agnes,' he said. 'And Edwin Leeford was my father.'

'Yes, dear heart,' Agnes said. 'Do you see now? You are both warlock and Knight and all the more powerful for it. Oliver, there is nothing you cannot do – nothing. You need only put your mind to it. Now you must wake up.'

'But what about you?' Oliver asked fearfully.

'Tell me that you will take on your mantle, that you will be the scourge of evil and one day close the door to hell. If you can tell me, that my soul will be at rest. I will be able to leave this place and go to Edwin.'

The woodcutter was just a few steps away from them now, his axe cutting a path through the water as he trailed it after him.

Oliver's eyes widened. He recognised the emerald set into the axe's handle – it was an Axe of the Darvish.

'I promise,' Oliver said. 'I promise you, I will close hell's door.'

'I love you, dear heart.' His mother kissed his cheek and began to fade.

'I love you, too,' Oliver said.

'Be good, always be good,' came Agnes's whispered words, and then she was gone.

The woodcutter loomed over Oliver with eyes that had only a pinprick of black. 'Hello, little sapling,' the axeman said.

He raised his weapon and the blade came slashing down.

Chapter XXIV

The pursuit and escape

Near to that part of the Thames where the buildings on the banks are dirtiest, and the vessels on the river blackest with coal dust, exists the filthiest, the strangest and the most extraordinary of the many places that are hidden in London. To reach this location, Bill Sikes, the wolfman, had to penetrate a maze of close, narrow and muddy streets, thronged by the roughest and poorest of waterside people. Here he had thought he might be safe. But he was wrong. Here he was still being pursued.

He could hear the shouts and clatter of feet in the distance. The Knights of Nostradamus had been on his trail for two hours now. He did not how they had found him, but now he was in their sights he couldn't seem to shake them.

The Knights were close and the wolfman knew he had to get off the street, go somewhere where they might not think to seek him.

With an unconscious Oliver over his shoulder, he made his way with difficulty along the narrow alleys which branched off on the right and left. Bullseye led the way, his paws scrabbling on the slippery cobbles.

Arriving, at length, in streets remoter and less frequented than those through which he had passed, the wolfman walked beneath tottering housefronts projecting over the pavement, dismantled walls that seemed to sway as he passed, chimneys half crushed and half hesitating to fall, and windows guarded by rusty iron bars that time and dirt had almost eaten away.

In front of him stood Jacob's Island, surrounded by a muddy ditch, six or eight feet deep and fifteen or twenty wide when the tide was in. On the island, the warehouses were roofless and empty; the walls were crumbling down; the windows were windows no more.

The wolfman crossed the bridge and stepped through the door of one of the old warehouses. He had chosen well. The door still had a key in its lock that he swiftly turned. The windows had also been lined with sheet iron and looked solid.

He threw Oliver to the ground as if he were an empty

sack and found a board which he set firmly against the door as a barricade. Here he would be safe.

Oliver leapt back, the axe missing his head by a finger's breadth. His whole body began to shake.

The woodcutter laughed. 'Little sapling, look how you quake. And you've been left all alone. Where has she gone?' The axeman turned his head, the dripping red tips of his hair catching the light. 'Too many years she has evaded my blade.'

'She's gone,' Oliver replied, hating the quiver in his voice. 'She's left this place. If you want to cut someone down, you'll need to come after me.'

The woodcutter lazily dragged his axe through the bog water. Backwards and forwards the blade went, stirring up thick silt from the bottom of the mire. 'You'll do, little sapling,' he said. 'I'll cut you down bit by bit, until there is nothing left. Nothing left at all.

Nothing. The word echoed in Oliver's head and the memory of his mother's voice came to him. *There is nothing you cannot do . . . You are both warlock and Knight . . .*

Oliver watched as the axe was drawn up from the water and lifted above the woodcutter's head. And a plan began to form.

'Is that an Axe of the Darvish?' Oliver asked.

The woodcutter stopped. 'Yes, what do you know of it?'

'I've fought with an Axe of the Darvish before,' Oliver said with a sigh. 'I found it rather tedious, if I'm honest. A weapon unworthy of my time.'

'Then I doubt it could have been a real Axe of the Darvish,' the woodcutter growled.

'It was,' Oliver insisted. 'It looked just like yours. Bigger perhaps.'

'Come now, little sapling, do you expect me to believe you could even lift this axe?'

'Believe what you will,' Oliver said. 'You slay the defenceless – it makes sense that the axe you treasure would be as pitiable as you are cowardly.'

The woodcutter laughed and thrust the handle of his axe out to Oliver. 'Sapling, if you can lift this weapon even an inch off the ground, I will spare your life. Would you call me a coward then?'

Oliver reached up for the weapon. His fingers grazed the skin of the woodcutter's hand, which felt cold and wet like the underbelly of a fish. As Oliver touched the wood of the axe's handle, he felt a familiar tension return to his arms. The Axe of the Darvish was lending him strength just as it had in the Knights' Armoury, when he had been training with Brownlow. Oliver knew that with a flick of his wrist, he could slay the woodcutter where he stood with his own blade.

Your father used his dark for good. The memory of his mother's words came to him again.

'And I will do the same.'

He would punish the woodcutter, but he would not slay a defenceless man. He let his arms go limp and the axe dangled into the water.

The woodcutter roared with laughter. 'You can't even keep it aloft.'

Oliver sighed deeply, as if defeated, and looked over his shoulder at the ring of stones.

The woodcutter followed his gaze. 'Those boulders can't protect you,' he mocked. 'You'll never make it in time.'

'I'm not going there,' Oliver responded. 'But your axe is.' Using all of the strength that the Axe of the Darvish gave him, Oliver threw the weapon towards the stones. Both boy and woodcutter watched as the axe sailed through the air before landing with a clatter within the ring of boulders.

The woodcutter let out a pained roar. 'What have you done?' He held his head in his bloodied hands. 'I'll never get it back and what am I without my axe? What am I? Nothing!' The man staggered towards the stones, the bog getting deeper and deeper as he went. As he got closer, his steps slowed until he could walk no further. It was as if the stones were pushing him back. With a sob, he dropped to his knees, the bog coming up to his chest, and he began to sink.

Oliver turned from the woodcutter. *It's time for me to wake up.*

Sikes could hear the Knights' voices, loud and earnest, the tramp of their hurried footsteps – endless they seemed in number – crossing the wooden bridge that would bring them on to the tiny island and towards the warehouse where he hid.

Hauling Oliver over his shoulder, Sikes climbed the stairs of the ramshackle building until he was on the very roof. He could see London spread out before him and also had clear sight of his pursuers.

There were about twenty-five of them, all dressed in the tunics of the Knights and bearing torches aloft. A man on horseback seemed to lead the crowd that had surrounded the warehouse. Sikes narrowed his eyes and saw that it was Brownlow and riding behind him in the saddle was Dodge. The wolfman growled, now knowing who had alerted the Knights.

From over his shoulder, Oliver suddenly let out a groan. And Sikes allowed himself a small smile. He was to have his revenge at least.

Some sixth sense alerted Brownlow and he looked up at the roof. He stared straight at Sikes.

'We're coming for you, Wolfman,' Brownlow called. 'Don't think you can get away.' He turned to the Knights. 'Hold your fire, he has Oliver. But get into that warehouse; rip it up from its foundations if you must.'

'Damn you!' cried the wolfman. 'Do your worst! I'll cheat you yet!'

Oliver opened his eyes to see the tiles of a roof and an army of Knights far below. He could see Grimwig with a bow and arrow over his shoulder, and there was Brownlow on a horse with Dodge behind him. Oliver's chest filled with relief that the man he now knew to be his grandfather was alive. *But where am I?*

He turned his gaze and saw the back of Sikes's head, then spotted Bullseye on the edge of the parapet.

'Put me down.' Oliver kicked out with his legs, but his time asleep had left his body very weak.

'Awake, are you?' the wolfman growled. 'That is fine with me. We have a reckoning, young Oliver.'

There came a loud thumping at the door, and then a hoarse murmur from such a multitude of angry voices as would have made the boldest quail. 'He's here! Break down the door!' Strokes, thick and heavy, rattled upon the door and lower window-shutters.

'In Nostradamus's name,' cried the voices. They arose again and again, each time louder. 'Break down the door!'

Oliver allowed himself to laugh. 'I think it is you who is about to have your reckoning, Bill Sikes.'

The wolfman crept over the tiles and looked over the low parapet. The water was out and the ditch a bed of mud. He sprang to his feet, determined to make one last effort for his life by dropping into the ditch and, at the risk of being stifled, endeavouring to creep away in the darkness and confusion. But as he stood on the edge, poised to jump, Bullseye began to yip. Sikes, realising the leap would end fatally, stepped back.

The crowd had been hushed during these few moments, watching the wolfman's motions and doubtful of his purpose. The instant they perceived it and knew it was defeated, they raised a cry of triumphant execration to which all their previous shouting had been whispers. Again and again it rose.

On pressed the Knights from the front – on, on, on, in a strong, struggling current of angry faces, with here and there a glaring torch to light them up and show them in all their wrath and passion.

'We have him now,' cried a Knight on the nearest bridge.

Roused into new strength and energy, and stimulated by the noise within the house that announced that an entrance had been made, Sikes lifted a struggling Oliver above his head. 'If I die, so do you,' he said. 'This is all your fault. I killed Nancy because of you.'

Oliver closed his eyes, Nancy's face filling his mind. He tried to call on the Rage, but sadness or the key held his powers prisoner.

Sikes's arms twitched. Oliver knew the wolfman was getting ready to hurl him and he began to struggle even more, knowing he was fighting for his life.

At that moment, Sikes froze and uttered a yell of terror. 'The eyes!' he cried in an unearthly screech. 'Nancy, do not look at me like that.'

Oliver turned his head. He could see a malevolent force streaked with purple and green hovering in front of Sikes. It twisted and turned, from mist to Nancy to mist again. With an inhuman screech, the purple blur sped towards Sikes and smote him full in the chest. Staggering as if struck by lightning, he took a step back and released Oliver from his grip.

Oliver cried out as he tumbled over the parapet, air rushing across his face, tiles ripping his clothes and skin as he went. A trailing length of cord that hung from a decrepit chimney stack flashed past him as he fell and he grabbed on to it. The rope ran with his weight, tight as a bowstring and swift as the arrow it sped. He fell for thirty-five feet, the cord burning then cutting into his hand. There was a sudden jerk, and the rope held fast. The old chimney quivered with the shock, but stood it bravely. Oliver smashed against a wall, but managed to keep his grip.

'Oliver, stay there.' It was Brownlow's voice from down below.

Oliver shook his head. 'I can't let Sikes escape,' he cried out. Gritting his teeth, he began to climb the rope, his muscles screaming in protest.

Bullseye, who had lain concealed till now, saw Oliver's approach. The wolf ran backwards and forwards on the parapet and let out a howl to warn Sikes. But Sikes was paying his brother little attention and stood motionless on the roof.

Bullseye made a decision. He collected himself for a spring and jumped for Oliver's throat. But Oliver was quicker. He kicked out against the wall and, as he swung back, Bullseye missed his aim and fell towards the ditch. The wolf turned over completely as he went and struck his head against a stone, dashing out his brains.

Oliver continued to climb. As he reached the parapet, he saw that Bill Sikes was standing quite still, teeth gritted. His furious eyes found Oliver's. 'The wisp is inside me,' he said. 'Nance is inside me.' The wolfman began to buck and jolt. His arms were suddenly flung out and fixed in position, like a scarecrow strapped to a wooden frame. He threw back his head and cried out in agony as his body went quite stiff. There was a crack of bones and the sound of tearing flesh, and then Sikes blew apart.

Gore splattered Oliver's face, warm and wet, and bones with tendons still attached skittered across the roof tiles and fell into the ditch below. Oliver wiped his eyes clear to see Nancy's wisp seething before him. She floated in the air, surrounded by flames of ghostly green and purple.

Her face was quite distorted with fury, but he could just about recognise the old Nancy in her features. Her red dress swirled about her, but her green boots were nowhere to be seen for her feet were bare and hung limply, as if her ankles had been broken. Nancy's arms stuck out like matchsticks and her hands dangled limply from her wrists.

'Nancy,' Oliver whispered and in that word, everything was said.

She opened her mouth into a deathly screech to show a tongue that was black as tar. She shifted into mist and surged towards him. Oliver tried to find the Rage, but he knew he was never going to be fast enough. At any moment, he expected to feel Nancy's wisp slam into his body and begin to tear him apart, but instead he felt a heaviness in the key round his neck. It vibrated on his chest and then exploded, shards flying like bullets.

Nancy stood in front of him again, swirling and seething. 'Give me peace, Oliver,' she begged. 'Use your power and give me peace.'

Oliver nodded, and remembering the woe-begottens in the graveyard, began to draw symbols on the air. Nancy smiled. Finally, all sorrow and pain were gone from her face and Oliver realised how young she had been.

'Thank you,' Nancy said. 'Be happy.' And her spirit flooded with light and was then gone altogether.

'Nice work, mate,' said a voice from behind.

Oliver turned to see Dodge, his body in the process of changing from smoke to flesh and blood. He looked ashen and a massive gash stretched across his forehead, but a wide grin split his face.

'Thanks.' Oliver played with the string that had once held the keeper's key. 'What are you doing here?'

'I was the one that brought Brownlow and the Knights.' Dodge explained. 'Sikes thought he'd killed me, but he didn't quite manage it.'

'I'm glad he didn't,' Oliver said with a smile.

'I'm sorry,' Dodge said. 'For everything that happened to you.'

Oliver held out a hand. 'Let's start again. My name is Oliver Twisted and I am more than a boy. I am a warlock and a Knight.'

Dodge grinned. 'My name is Jack Dawkins and I am a smoke-shifter and a future apprentice to the Knights of Nostradamus. Come on, mate, I'll take you down. I know Brownlow is keen to see you.'

Oliver took Dodge's hand and they turned to smoke.

Chapter XXV

And last

The fortunes of those who have figured in this tale are nearly closed. The little that remains to their historian to relate is told in few and simple words.

Oliver Twisted was reunited with Mr Brownlow and the truth was quickly shared that Brownlow was in fact Oliver's grandfather. Brownlow wept tears of joy and promised to raise and nurture Oliver with all the love and care that Agnes would have bestowed if she were still alive.

As this is an honest account of the life and fortunes of Oliver Twisted, it must be said that this nurture manifested itself in the form of a Knight's tunic, intensive training in the magical arts, hand-to-hand combat and many lessons in which Oliver was taught how to read and how to harness the Rage.

During his apprenticeship as a Knight of Nostradamus, Oliver was exposed to all manner of beast and foe. Mrs Bedwin complained most bitterly about this, but the boy had never been happier.

Dodge collected what little possessions he had from Fagin's den and took up residence with Oliver, Brownlow and Mrs Bedwin. He too became an apprentice to the Knights of Nostradamus. Dodge and Oliver became good friends, indeed, more like brothers.

Together the two boys vowed to stop the evil that blighted the lives of innocents. Together they would close the Night Markets and bloodfarms of this world, but to do that they would have to become strong and skilled. They would have to become the most accomplished Knights that had ever trodden the earth, for their victory could only be achieved if they defeated evil at the very highest seats of power.

Dodge often worried that Fagin might summon him via the keeper's key that still hung round his neck and so, after much research, Grimwig found the tools to cut the key from Dodge's neck. The boy was now free of Fagin, but the soul-stealer had long disappeared into the night with his band of thieves and had not been seen since. Both the Knights of Nostradamus and the Brotherhood of Fenris were keen to ascertain his whereabouts, but Fagin had hidden himself very well indeed.

Grimwig and Dodge had managed to form a strong friendship during the cutting of the key and the irritable old gentleman became Dodge's mentor. Dodge accordingly visited Grimwig a great many times in the course of a year. On all such occasions, Grimwig showed Dodge many different ways in which it was possible to see the truth of a person – be it with a spyglass or some other divination. He continued to do everything in a very singular and unprecedented manner, but always maintained his favourite assertion, that his mode was the right one and that he had always known that Oliver could be trusted.

Toby Crackit, appalled by the murder of Nancy, fell into a train of reflection as to whether an honest life was not after all the best. Arriving at the conclusion that it certainly was, he turned his back upon the scenes of the past and resolved to mend his ways in some new sphere of action. He struggled hard and suffered much for some time, but having a determined disposition, found his way to Northamptonshire and is now the merriest farmer in all the county, his tentacles finding the work on the farm to be easy enough.

And now the hand that traces these words falters, as it approaches the conclusion of its task, and would weave, for a little longer space, the thread of these adventures.

Hell's door was still open, darkness still resided in the

heart of the kingdom, but it is fair to say that the agents of evil were scared. For when they looked upon the future, they saw a prophecy come true. They saw Oliver Twisted, his face full of fury and eyes molten silver with power, cast each and every one of them back into hell and close the door.

Each night, the Brotherhood of Fenris sat round their table and Lord Skinim planned ways to bring about Oliver's demise, but nothing seemed able to change the course of the future. And so it came to be that it was not the children of the bloodfarm who had nightmares, but Lord Skinim. For a change was coming and there was nothing he could do about it . . .

A Note from the Author

Why did I write *Oliver Twisted*? Well, once the title had popped into my head, how could I not? What delicious potential the idea had. Taking a story as well known as *Oliver Twist* and giving it a new, much darker reality was just so appealing I had to do it.

I have always loved *Oliver Twist*. The book, the musical or cartoon, you name it – I've read it or watched it. I've always thought how awesome it was that Dickens chose to show us a face of Victorian England that no other writer of the age was really brave enough or interested enough to do.

The idea that innocents are born into a hellish world is very much at the heart of *Oliver Twist* and I wanted to keep that at the centre of *Oliver Twisted*. However, I also wanted to take this sense of hell even further and create a society where demons live side by side with humans and where dark forces sit in the highest seats of power.

Storytelling is about wanting to add your voice, your ideas, to the millions that have gone before. It is about wanting to find new ways to delight, terrify and surprise.

Oliver Twist was an amazing starting point for *Oliver Twisted* because the original story is so well known. I think this familiarity means that some of the journeys I have taken the characters on end up being even more surprising.

I hope you enjoyed the journey as much as I did and thanks to Charles Dickens for the map . . .

A Conversation with JD Sharpe

If I suspect that someone is a warlock, what should I do?
Run for it and hope the warlock is too busy plotting how they are going to take over the world to come after you.

Family excluded, who is one person (living, dead, fictional, etc) that you'd want at your side to fight off a woe-begotten horde? What would be your weapon of choice?
I'd have Katniss Everdeen from *The Hunger Games* as she is exactly the kind of person you want by your side in a tight spot. My weapon of choice would be phenomenal martial arts moves.

Woe-begottens are laying siege to your house. You only have time to grab three things before you enter a secret underground chamber. What do you take?
1. A box set of *American Dad* (am going to assume I have a DVD player).
2. A bottle of Tabasco sauce. I imagine that I'm only going to have tinned food to eat and chilli sauce makes most things taste better. A bottle of Tabasco can also double up as a weapon.

3. My laptop. I sometimes get distracted when writing. With woe-begottens outside my door I bet I'd get down to work . . .

Be honest: who's your favourite character in *Oliver Twisted*? Is there any character in particular that you identify with?

Oliver is obviously the hero of the novel and so he has lots of traits that I admire and kind of wish I had – for example he is pretty fearless and selfless, and he has that whole magic thing going on. Oliver also has serious backbone and is ultimately pretty stubborn, which I can empathise with just a tiny bit.

I also have a soft spot for Dodge. He has been exposed to many horrors during his short life and has had to develop a really thick skin to survive. Despite all this, he manages to hang on to his humanity and when the time comes he shows his courage and his true nature, which is brave and good. Also he can turn into smoke which would be a pretty useful skill to have at times.

Oliver Twisted has some disturbing imagery and situations in them. Where do you get your ideas?

To be honest, I don't really know where I get my ideas from. If I was going to analyse it I think I tend to be inspired by events and images from the real world.

The whole idea of bloodfarms came from the fact that historically the weakest in society have often been exploited for the gain of the most powerful in society. This knowledge led me to an idea of a farm where children were reared for their blood. I often get inspiration from other books or movies. And when I am really stuck I try and dream an answer.

Do you have any little quirks when you are writing?
No, I can write anywhere, although I much to prefer to write with music on in the background. I have different playlists for different moods. My 'peril' playlist has Jay Z and Beethoven on it. I also like chewing gum. It helps me think, but is extremely annoying for others if I am working in a public place.

Aside from writing, what is the one talent you wish you had?
I wish I could sing. Unfortunately I can't. But that doesn't stop me. That's true horror.

Do you have a good luck charm?
They are not exactly charms, but I collect antique keys. I love keys because they open doors, and an open door is the beginning of a story.

Would you like some gore more?

Woe-begottens at your door?

Team Twist or Team Twisted?

You decide at **www.olivertwisted.co.uk**

Photo by Amanda Herbert

JD Sharpe grew up in London, went to Oxford University, and for a whole summer thought about becoming a police officer and so worked at New Scotland Yard. JD finally decided that writing horror stories would be far more exciting, and creating villains more fun than actually capturing them.

To get in touch please visit www.jdsharpe.co.uk

To find out more about other fantastic books
for young adult readers check out the brilliant new
ELECTRIC MONKEY website:

Trailers

Blogs

News and Reviews

Competitions

Downloads

Free stuff

Author interviews

 Like us on Facebook

Follow us on Twitter

WWW.ELECTRICMONKEYBOOKS.CO.UK